The Paper Men

also by William Golding

LORD OF THE FLIES

THE INHERITORS

PINCHER MARTIN

BRASS BUTTERFLY (play)

FREE FALL

THE SPIRE

THE HOT GATES

THE PYRAMID

THE SCORPION GOD

DARKNESS VISIBLE

RITES OF PASSAGE

A MOVING TARGET

WILLIAM GOLDING

The Paper Men

faber and faber

LONDON·BOSTON

First published in 1984
by Faber and Faber Limited
3 Queen Square London WC1N 3AU
Photoset and printed in Great Britain by
Redwood Burn Limited
Trowbridge, Wiltshire

© William Golding, 1984

British Library Cataloguing in Publication Data

Golding, William
The paper men
I. Title
823'.914[F]   PR6013.035

ISBN 0–571–13206–5

For
my friend and publisher
CHARLES MONTEITH

Chapter I

I knew at once that it was one of those nights. The drink, such as it had been, was dying out of my brain and leaving a kind of sediment of irritation, vague discomfort and even remorse. It had not been—no, indeed—a *bender* or *booze-up*. By the exercise of special pleading I could have persuaded other people that my evening's consumption had been no more than reasonable with regard to the duties of a host: an English author entertaining a professor of English Literature from overseas. I could also have pleaded that it had been my fiftieth birthday and that we had been having, quote, one of those long, continental meals that are at the heart of European civilization, unquote. (Come to think of it I don't know if that's a quote or not. Call it a clitch.) But the indefatigable analyst of my character—myself, that is—would have none of it. There had been those drinks at lunch. They were the fatal first step, implying in themselves a desert period between four and five o'clock when one would feel not justified but urged, shoved, compelled by the process started at midday to bring the six o'clock hour of offering the guest a drink back to five o'clock, which in its turn—and so on. If I could congratulate myself on a degree of sobriety at half-past three in the morning, it was a minuscule triumph that most people would have considered a defeat.

And boring young Professor Rick L. Tucker would be there at breakfast! At the memory of him I started up in bed, then collapsed again with a groan. It was a small blessing to count, that he had no wife with him, or I should probably have made a pass at her or at the very least been suggestive. And we should drink again. No. *I* should drink again, out of opportunity and boredom, thus making a nonsense of the high moral stand, the teetotalism that had seemed so irrefrangible no longer ago than last Monday.

There was another thing. It was a black hole in my memory of the previous night, where the long summer evening had turned into night. It was not a large black hole—merely a blotch between the after-dinner drinking and—yes, now it was smaller, the black hole I mean, because on its very brink I remembered getting up yet another bottle, opening it, despite their protests and—doing what? I examined my throat, my mouth, my head, my stomach. It was impossible to believe that I had really made any significant inroads into that (fifth?) bottle. Otherwise my head would be . . . and my stomach would be . . . and the black hole would be. . . .

It was at that very moment—and if I bothered to leaf through that pile of journals out there that I am going to burn, I could tell you the hour as well as the date—that I conceived a thought. The point where drinking can be defined as alcoholism is precisely where the black hole is recognized as part of it. I remember thinking, in the terrible clarity of early morning, that the symptoms also implied that the disease was incurable. For it was part of the running of the mind, the universal process. I sat up in bed, but slowly. The window was aglimmer. I moved into another emotional gear, another symptom, perhaps, a feeling of dry, hard factuality that probed my situation from every side, an army of unutterable law which in time might produce unthinkable horrors, as in all accounts of drug addiction. It was not impossible to envisage this very dryness and bleakness as a monster itself that was not yet visible—and would not, I thought with a spurt of real desperation, would not ever *be* visible if I could help it! I would fight the black hole, fight it on the beaches, in pubs and restaurants, clubs, bars, in travel, in the house, in the very damned delectable bottles themselves, hoping at last to find some pleasure without payment or, alternatively, a pleasure taken in calm, sober daylight rather than this stare so dry and hard—I was frightened, I remember, in a deep, hard way, an appalled way. No, no, I protested to the glimmering window, it can't be as bad as that! But the words of the wise man returned upon me. Remember that everything that can happen to a man can happen to you!

I took hold of myself. There is no such thing as universal insurance. Black hole there might be, but the first thing a bitterly sobering man would do would be to probe it, find a light to shine here and there until the hole was seen to be no more than a case of forgetfulness that must increase with the advance, year by year, of middle age. My sanity told me that there was a tool to hand. I had only to go downstairs, examine the four empty bottles and the fifth partly empty one, look round in the spirit of Holmes or of Maigret and reconstruct that period between dinner and bed from the evidence of glasses and bottles, spilt booze it might be, or perhaps mercifully not and I should find the fifth bottle still full with no more than a cork drawn—

At that, I heard Elizabeth turn over in the other bed with a sleeper's sigh. She would know—oh, yes indeed! Doubtless I should hear all in bad time; but why wake her and ask? The way to discover the truth was to creep down in dressing-gown and slippers, yes, and with the pocket torch which I kept at the ready by my bed because our area is notorious for power failures. Nor must I be fobbed off by any drunken efforts on my own part to conceal the evidence. I must interrogate the bottles. If it proved necessary, I must sneak out of the back door—no, the conservatory was quieter—get to the dustbin, ashcan, *poubelle*, whatever one chose to call it and, not to elaborate, count the empties. For the truth was that already I did not believe in the bottle still full but with the cork drawn. That would be a miracle and miracles, though they might happen, did not seem to apply to me. Yet, so enfeebled was I in mind rather than body that the thought of waking Elizabeth accidentally turned the prospect of getting out of bed into a test of will power like diving into cold water. I have never liked cold water.

It was at this moment that my wavering mind was made up for me. The rubberized lid of the dustbin outside the back door fell off. Somehow that made the whole issue clear. I was no longer a repentant drinker. I was Outraged Householder. *Sir, how much longer in the guise of enlightened conservationism are we to endure the depredations of these clumsy creatures and at the same time run the risk of contamination by a disease once thought eradicated? Sir, while we must be mindful, sir—sir, sir, sir—*

Bloody badgers. I twisted out of bed, hardly minding whether Elizabeth woke or not. The only gun in my house was an ancient but powerful airgun which I had acquired with a tin of pellets through circumstances too trivial and complex to be worth recording. Author—no, well-known author—no, damn it, Wilfred Barclay shoots badger. Was there a law against it? Something dating from King John or thereabouts? Could you not shoot a badger on your own land? My head was quite extraordinarily uncluttered, my hangover marvellously pushed into the background. I felt pardoned. Perhaps it was the possibility of killing something, the countryman's hereditary privilege. I bundled into my dressng-gown, shoved on my slippers. Stealthily I stole down the stairs, past the room where our guest slept his solitary sleep in the *letto matrimoniale* of the spare room. I fished the gun out of the cupboard by the dining-room fireplace, cocked and loaded it. I tiptoed into the warm conservatory, opened the door and peered round the corner.

Here was a dilemma. How do you shoot a badger when you can make it out as no more than an enlargement of a dustbin? The creature had its paws on the rim, its head down, as it searched nastily and avidly through our rubbish. It would be licking at scraps of pâté and perhaps gnawing old bacon rind or the bone from a gammon. It was wild nature and probably gassable but only by the appropriate authorities. Then again (*was* there a chill in the air for all the time of the year?) were badgers dangerous—not only by transmitting disease, but actively, toothily, clawily dangerous? Would a wounded badger attack? Would a tickled-up badger or one with young (were there young with it?) go for my throat? The situation was not simple and was further complicated by the absurd. I was wearing an old pair of pyjamas and the cord of my dressing-gown was gripping me a little above where the pyjamas should have been gripping me but were too ancient for their elasticated top to do so. They were performing as they always did, even in contrary conditions. If I was losing weight, they slipped down. If I was gaining weight, they slipped down. I had the loaded gun in one hand, my torch in the other and no third hand for my trousers which now fell suddenly under my dressing-gown so that I only just caught them by clapping my knees together. It was, perhaps, no situation from which to face a charging badger. I recognized uneasily the hand of what I sometimes thought to be my personal nemesis, the spirit of farce.

There came a fresh sound from the dustbin. I began to shuffle forward in a complex manner, the gun in one hand, the other hand partly holding the torch in my pocket and at the same time hooked into my trouser top. A sudden breeze rattled the branches noisily in the orchard. I reached the dustbin at the exact moment when the badger, it may be, alarmed by the sudden sound, froze in its probing act. I faced it across the bin. The badger looked up and uttered the only really "strangled cry" I have ever experienced outside fiction. This cry was the beginning of a high sound expressed in the funnies as *glug* or *gulp*. The dawn-lit face of Professor Rick L. Tucker rose before me beyond the further rim. I ought to have been embarrassed for him but I wasn't. He had bored me and intruded, he had shown every sign of prying, of making a professional meal of me. Now I had caught him in the act of the unthinkable. I spoke very loudly. If this woke up the whole world, I implied by my decibels, why should I conceal the fact that I had found a full professor of Eng. Lit. rifling my dustbin?

11

"You must be very hungry, Tucker. I'm sorry we didn't feed you better."

He made no sound at all. I could see the kitchen door was open behind him. I had no free hand with which to point. I gestured with the airgun and that commanding gesture tightened my finger (unaccustomed enough to guns, these days) round the trigger. The gun went off with a report that in daytime would have seemed no louder than a cork popping but in the dawn sounded like the first shot of D Day. Tucker may have given another strangled cry for all I know, but all I heard was the shot, its echo and the cries of what sounded like all the birds for miles. Tucker turned and moved clumsily as a badger into the kitchen. I hobbled after him, switched on the light, shut the door and stood the gun beside it. I sank on to a stool on one side of the kitchen table and, as if an interview or a continuation of the last one was inevitable, Tucker sank on to a stool across the table from me. My own farcical situation and incompetence changed my irritation into fury.

"For God's sake, Tucker!"

There was a smear of some food or other on his cheek, marmalade and a tealeaf or two on the back of his hand. It was evident how he had rummaged—even opening the plastic bags that were put out to catch the dustmen or, as Tucker might say, the Sanitary Engineers, in what I usually called our village festival. Tucker's right hand held a mass of rumpled paper, papers I had thought disposed of safely only twenty-four hours before. There was a torn scrap of paper hanging on his bedrobe, a scrap with childish scrawls of writing on it.

"God, Tucker, you are the most— Do you suppose I throw away—? Well—"

I remembered with sudden unease. It wasn't that simple.

"What you've got there, Tucker, is what's commonly called fan mail. I don't get much but what I do get is worth less than a good honest toilet roll. You can take

12

one of those with you if you like."

"Please, Wilf—"

"And you've cut yourself. There's broken glass in that dustbin."

He rocked on the stool.

"Shot. . . ."

It was like hearing a strangled cry for the first time. It was like hearing the word "shot" for the first time.

"Christ!"

I leapt to my feet, took a step and grabbed the table to save myself. My pyjama trousers fell round my ankles. I kicked them off as the ghastly seriousness of the situation flashed in on me. It was a peripeteia to end all peripeteias. From being indignantly in the right I was now monstrously in the wrong.

"Here. Let me see."

"No, no. I'll be OK."

"Nonsense, man—here!"

"Guess I'll make out.'

I grabbed the belt of his bedrobe, pulled the knot loose, then dragged the whole thing down from his shoulders. A densely hairy chest came into view, then a narrower shrubbery leading down to an even more densely haired nest of privates.

"Where is it, for God's sake?"

He said nothing but swayed. The bedrobe dragged down his arm from thick upper arm to thick forearm. I nerved myself for the bloody revelation. I got the bedrobe down to his wrist. There was a bruise on it and a scratch. A trickle of blood led down to the back of his hand.

"Tucker, you fool, you're not hurt at all!"

As if on cue the kitchen door opened, stage left. Elizabeth came in, surveyed Tucker's hairy nakedness and my discarded pyjama trousers.

"I don't want to be fussy but it is rather late and extremely difficult to get to sleep or stay there. Could you two men make less noise about it?"

"About what, Liz?"

"About whatever you're doing."

"Can't you see? I shot him. He was at the dustbin, ashcan, trashcan. The badger— Oh God, I can't explain!"

Elizabeth smiled with terrible sweetness. "I've no doubt you will, given a little time, Wilfred."

"I thought he was a badger. I fired the airgun accidentally, you see—"

"Yes, I do see," said Elizabeth charmingly. "Well if you are going to continue, please don't frighten the horses."

"Liz!"

She bent down and picked up a scrap of paper that had fallen from Tucker somewhere. With one hand up to her hair she turned the paper over, read it silently at first, then aloud.

". . . longing to be with you. Lucinda."

She turned the paper over again and sniffed it with delicate connoisseurship. "And who is Lucinda?"

Then, as if she had switched channels, she became the perfect hostess. She had to be assured that Tucker's now concealed hairiness had not suffered. She indicated that the whole thing was the sort of joke she was used to and enjoyed. Quite soon she left us still sitting at the table. My hangover was back, increased and only made endurable by the depth of fury I felt.

"I wish to God I *had* shot you!"

Tucker nodded submissively, willing to be shot in the cause of scholarship, even conceding my right to do it, marvellous me. He was prepared to concede my wonderful right of control over everything in the wide world except the words I had written or received, which were by their nature, no, by my nature—oh, what the hell? Even now I can remember my hatred of Tucker, apprehension over Liz and anger with impossible, daft Lucinda. Stir into that fury with myself and sheer blazing rage at the farcical improbability and implacability of the Fact. Beyond all the contrivances of paper, manipulations of plot, delineation of character, dénouements and resolutions, there, in that real world, real dustbin, the

14

quite implausible actions of individuals had brought into the light of day a set of circumstances I had thought concealed from the relevant person and finally disposed of. Nor, in all this, had I the comfort of any morality, only immorality.

"Tucker."

"You were calling me Rick, Wilf."

'Listen, Tucker. Tomorrow you were leaving. I mean today. You are never coming back. Never, never, never, never, never."

"You make me deeply unhappy, Wilf."

"Go to bed, for God's sake!"

I put my elbows on the table and my forehead in my hands. All at once a black despair descended on me.

"Go to bed, go away, get out. Leave me alone, alone—"

He answered me out of the depths of his reverent absurdity.

"I understand, Wilf. It's the Burden."

At last the kitchen door closed. Sheer self-pity was filling the dark hollows behind my eyelids with water. Lucinda, Elizabeth, Tucker, the book that was going so badly—the water spilled into my palms the way the blood had trickled out of Tucker. In the trees the dawn chorus was in full, joyous swing.

Presently I opened my eyes. Yes, of course I should have known. The evidence had been staring me in the face. It stood by the sink, the bottle I had opened that I couldn't persuade anyone to drink. It was empty. By its side stood another one. That was empty too.

Immediately my hangover became desperate. I hunted about for pills, stole some of Liz's that had been effective before. By the back door the dustbin fell over. Furiously I staggered out. A black-and-white creature with a bristly back was running along by the river bank, making for the mill dam where it could cross into the woods opposite us. The dustbin, ashcan, trashcan, *poubelle*, the evidence, the incriminator, lay on its side with a trail of household rubbish, refuse, cartons, bottles, bits of meat, eggshells

15

strewn from it all the way along the wake of the badger; and in the mess, scribbled, typed, printed, black-and-white and coloured—paper, paper, paper!

It was too much. The village festival, that weekly collecting of all our yesterdays, must look after itself. I crept, as I thought, softly through the house. I opened the door of "our" bedroom, in blinding daylight. Elizabeth turned over.

"I'm not asleep."

"Look, Liz—"

"'Longing to be with you. Lucinda.'"

I was too miserable to speak. I gathered the eiderdown from my bed and found my way, half-blind, to the hole I sometimes call my study. The dawn chorus had died away and I knew that the sounds of Monday morning would begin long before my head was anywhere near rescued from ruin. It was at that—well, not moment but *juncture*—that I realized something not so much with a start as with a convulsion. There were torn photographs in the dustbin as well. *Why* had I gone through those boxes to rid myself of old shames, my past, and dumped them in the dustbin instead of burning them? *Why* had I told Tucker? *Why* was he such a dedicated, such a determined, single-minded fool? Somewhere in all that spilt rubbish, crumpled, torn, smeared with jam or fat—now there was no knowing who in the household, our daily, or out there, the dustmen, or milkman—or lying in a badger's stomach or its sett: the point was that Rick L. Tucker and a badger with their dawn antics had put me in danger of losing my wife and my dignity at the same time. The assiduity and humble determination that had seemed comic at first now seemed to threaten me like a disease. It was as if all paper had become sticky by nature so that whether it was lard or marmalade you could never rid yourself of the stuff, once committed to it. It was flypaper and I was the fly. It was the Venus Flytrap, the Sundew. It was those footsteps in the sands of time that I now saw I preferred not to leave behind me.

16

Chapter II

"And who is Lucinda?"

That was the beginning of the end of my marriage to Liz. Never marry a woman nearly ten years younger than yourself. It took years, what with the state of the law as touching divorce. We were and are and always shall be profoundly connected, not in love or hate, nor in the trite compromise of a *love/hate relationship*. Whatever it was, the thing was there, to be enjoyed, fought against and suffered. We were entirely unsuitable for each other and for making anything but a dissonance. As long as Liz stayed healthy she was integrated and moral. I lived in the simple conviction, I now see, that I could only remain integrated by immorality. This immorality carried in it the necessity of concealment—though who knows now what Liz knew or suspected? That dirty piece of paper was a catalyst. If I had been sufficiently aware, I might have seen in its appearance from the dustbin the corner of a pattern that was to prove itself universal. Lucinda pre-dated my marriage to Liz and at the time of the dustbin I was involved with a girl successfully concealed. Irony? The Eye of Osiris?

Caught in the kitchen with Rick L. Tucker and the piece of paper, I was led to do the one thing to which I was wholly unaccustomed; that is, I made a clean breast of everything. Contrary to all expectations (particularly as illustrated by novels), Elizabeth understood but did not forgive. On mature reflection (old man sitting in the sun), I think she only wanted the excuse. Our rows were fiercer than duels. We were sophisticated but uncivilized. I went and stayed at the sleazier of my clubs, telling her that she was welcome to the house, garden, paddocks, horses, cars, boat, limited company, *anything*, but I couldn't stand it any more. The club had a strict limit for the number of consecutive nights you could sleep there. So when I went home to be forgiven, I found she had gone off herself. She had left a note saying that I was welcome to the house, garden, paddock, horses, cars, boat, limited company, *anything*, but she couldn't stand it any more.

Even then we might have come together and continued our necessary wrangle until age and indifference had granted us a mutual sense of humour. But that horsy creature Capstone Bowers appeared on the horizon. Julian sorted it all out in time—the goods and chattels and messuage or whatever it is—and the marriage came to as much of an end as any marriage of that length ever does. The only damaged party, I think, was our poor little Emily. I met Humphrey Capstone Bowers only once, by appointment, at that same sleazy club, the Random. They—we—are an odd lot and connected with paper, from advertising and children's comics all the way through to pornography. You might say that apart from me our most celebrated member is Anon. Capstone Bowers looked down his nose at the crowd—he must be the last Englishman to wear a monocle—and muttered that he hadn't seen such a lot, ever. Pressed severely by me, he remarked that we were all *rather bush*. To give you a completer picture of the man, he shot big game all over the world and targets at Bisley. Towards the end of our brief conversation which we were holding to, as he said, "sort things out", I was building myself up to the point where I would employ my ample linguistic resources to tell him what I thought of him, when he said with the simplicity of absolute candour, "You know, Barclay, you're such a shit." You can see the sort of man he was. I mean.

Well.

Freedom at fifty-three! What nonsense. What *bloody*

nonsense! Freedom was what faced me. My advice is, don't try it. If you see it coming, run. Or if it tempts you to run, stay put. Believe it or not, my head was full of anticipated sex, and with imagined girls young enough to be my granddaughters, very nearly. That may have been why I didn't mind Capstone Bowers moving in with Liz one little bit. It was nothing to do with our unbreakable, unbearable connection. Poor little Emily minded. She ran away and had to be fetched back by the police. I could understand her bolting. From what I've heard since, even the horses hated Capstone Bowers.

I moved about. I had many acquaintances but few friends. I stayed with one or two of them. One even produced a woman but she proved to be a serious academic and a structuralist to boot. God, I might as well have shacked up with Rick L. Tucker!

I moved to Italy and irony at once took charge, for I chummed up with an Italian woman of near enough my own age and more or less in a pass of the windy Apennines, like the man said. I was fond of her, I suppose, but what kept me there for more than two years was a *piano nobile* like a museum and servants who hid their sneers. I was so chuffed, I remember—oh Barclay, Barclay, what a snob you are!—I rang Elizabeth and got Emily out to me for a bit. She hated Italy, the place, my Italian chum and, I'm still sorry to say, me. So back she went, and we didn't meet again for years.

All this time, though I hardly noticed except as a small irritant, Professor Tucker kept sending letters which Elizabeth forwarded because it gave her an excuse to nag me about my papers. They were strewn through the house and increasing daily from one source or another. I ignored the letters. Only when she sent me a cable, FOR GODS SAKE WILF WHAT AM I TO DO WITH YOUR PAPERS, did I reply, BURN THE BLOODY LOT. But she never did. She took to nailing them up in tea chests and dumping them in the wine cellar. Outside a game reserve or a rifle range Capstone Bowers was such an ignorant sod he never grasped what they would be worth on the open market or, worse, on the closed one.

My Italian connection came to an end. The fact is that religion, in the shape of Padre Pio, had got to her. Out of curiosity we'd been to one of those dawn masses which always ended in a stampede of the faithful, anxious to get a glimpse of the man's stigmata before his helpers carried him away out of sight. I was a bit shocked to see that cool, civilized woman scrumming with the rest. She came back to me at last, her veil down and tears streaming behind it. Her voice was deep with a kind of triumphant grief.

"Now, can you doubt?"

That irritated me.

"All I saw was a poor old man being half-carried away from the altar. That was all!"

She said nothing more in the church, but the argument started again in the back of the car on the way "home". I know now that what was significant about my reaction as well as hers was the fact that we were involved, both of us, and driven to quarrel so bitterly. My driving force was a passionate need for there *not* to be a miracle.

"Look, it's all hysteria!"

"I saw them, I tell you, the wounds. God forgive us, we're not worthy even to speak the word!"

'Supposing you did see them, what does that prove?"

"There is no 'Supposing'."

"People can think themselves into these things. It's like a false pregnancy—every symptom there but no baby. Remember what I told you about when I was a bank clerk?"

"You are disgusting, Wilfred Barclay."

"And later on, years later. Look at that hand! I was hypnotized. I mean, I was literally, professionally hypnotized. At a party it was and in my, my—"

"Oh, I, I, my *my*—"

"*Will* you listen? Yes. Egotism. I didn't think anyone could do such a thing to me. And what happened?"

"I do not wish to talk about it."

20

"There, on the back on my hand, my own initials, flaming like scars, inflamed like burns—"

"I will not talk about it!"

(But the man knew. It was his triumph, his power. There was infuriating complacency in his smile. *You are very receptive to hypnotic suggestion, sir. Give Mr Barclay a big hand, ladies and gentlemen!*)

"Look, dear. You don't want to talk and I don't want to hurt you—but you see suggestion can do such things!"

"An old man bleeds for you day after day, year after year. He allows God to dispose of him in two places at once because his charity is too great for the resources of one, poor body—"

The extraordinary woman burst into tears.

After that, of course, we fought no more. It was a sort of truce, I suppose. I treated her with uncomprehending and heavy tact, staying out of her way as far as possible. She herself withdrew and became the perfect hostess like Liz. It's an awful effect to have on people. I wish women would throw things.

Even so, it might have turned out differently if my attention hadn't been taken up by another matter. I had to lecture. It's amusing in a way that a man whose education finished in the fifth should find himself mixed up so with scholars. The truth is that what began with my feeling flattered ended by boring me—and worse. As I say, I was sometimes called to lecture for my country's good. I did it obediently, at gatherings of academics. You see, though you can accuse Wilfred Barclay of being an ignorant sod with little Latin and less Greek, adept in several broken languages and far more deeply read in bad books than good ones, I have a knack. Academics had to admit that in the last analysis I was what they were about. I repeat there was nothing in it for me but a bit of flattery, a tiny, perhaps absurd, feeling that my country needed me and the occasional interest of an exotic place. It was a long time before the penny dropped. The penny was, of all things, of all people, the badger at the bin, Rick L. Tucker.

At the time of the row about stigmata, with my Italian chum behaving like a gracious lady, I was about to go to Spain. I debated pushing off without seeing her but rashly came to the conclusion that would make things worse. I wish now I had left in the dignity of silence.

"Well, I'll be going, then."

She did not turn completely to face me. She turned her head so that her profile was outlined against the worn tapestry. "It is enough."

"What is?"

"The two of us."

"Why?"

"It is enough. That's all."

I considered a number of inquiries. I meditated admitting the crudity of my response to Padre Pio and offering to go and give the poor old man a chance to convert me when I came back. Time, I thought, time was the great healer.

"When I come back we'll talk."

"Go! Go! Go!"

If that was not enough she followed it with a blast of Italian, gutter stuff I think, and of which I only got the general drift of her attitude to me, to Protestants, to men and to the English as I exemplified them.

So I took off for a conference in Seville at the old tobacco factory which chaps who know that sort of thing will remember is where Carmen waggled her hips, though now it's only a university. Mostly at conferences I keep away until the last day, when it's my turn to sound like an author. But the professor who had invited me, when asked if they had any Carmens still about said, "Yes, very many," so I went along, forgetting it would be out of termtime.

There at the podium I would grace later was Rick Tucker, larger than ever and reading from a huge manuscript. A sleepy bunch of professors, lecturers, postgraduate students were all trying their hardest to stay awake and Professor Tucker was making it difficult for them. I sank into a vacant chair at the back of the hall and composed myself to slumber.

What jerked me awake was the sound of my own name in Tucker's peculiarly toneless American. His head was down, and he was reading from the manuscript, and he was on about my relative clauses. He had counted them, apparently, book by book. He had made a graph, and if they consulted appendix twenty-seven among the goodies handed to them by the grace of the conference organizers, they would be able to find his graph there and follow his deductions. Here and there among the audience I saw heads nod, then jerk up again. A few females appeared to be taking notes. A male head fell back in front of me and a faint snore came from it. Prof. Tucker, still toneless, was now pointing out the significant difference between his graph and the one constructed by a Japanese Professor Hiroshige (that was what he sounded like), for Professor Hiroshige, it appeared, had not done his homework, to our surprise, and had also been guilty of the gross error of confusing my compound sentences with my complex ones. In fact Professor Hiroshige should get lost and leave the field to the acknowledged expert, who had heard from the author's own lips that he did not tolerate so overly broad an interpretation in his iconography of the absolute, or words to that effect.

I sat there, amused, and having my ego massaged gently, when Rick Tucker, while turning a page, chanced to glance up at his audience. It was the dustbin all over again. It was *glug* or *gulp*. From that moment his voice faded and his colour deepened. Listening intently, I could tell why. He was drawing his chin back into his collar. He was not the sort of man who finds it possible to depart from the text before him. The stream of typed words drew him along inexorably to where, in my hearing, he did not want to go. He claimed, I heard him mutter, a deep personal relationship with me and (what a more experienced academic would not have wished to have, knowing the slipperiness of that slope) my verbal

23

agreement with everything he was now telling his listless audience. Then, perhaps faced by some even more outrageous statement of our alleged intimacy, he tried to ad lib, turned two pages at once, then dropped the whole manuscript from the desk so that it glided and fluttered this way and that across the floor. It woke the audience and during that brief interlude I made an unseen exit. Next day I performed the party piece I was paid for and raked the audience for a sign of Rick, hoping to show him what could be done in the way of ad libbing round a man who claimed a deep personal relationship with me but he was nowhere to be found. I wonder why? Such sensitivity was not like him. Then the whole thing slipped from my mind because when I went back to Italy things took a steep dive into the absurd and I got the shock I was not prepared for. It was a mixture of quaintness, meanness and majestic lunacy. I was prepared to be dignified but forgiving about the plane not being met by a car; but the gate was shut, barred and locked. A green canvas wagon tilt just by the gate covered several suitcases all carefully, you might say lovingly, packed with my personal effects. How the servants must have sniggered. I sat in the taxi, a folder containing all the guff from the conference on the seat by me, and wondered where to go. It was an Italian come-uppance.

Fortunately *Coldharbour* kept on selling, as it still does, to say nothing of *All We Like Sheep*, and money was no problem. Neither, at that time, was invention, for I saw, leafing through the papers from the conference, that I had no need of it. Here, then, is what turns that whole mixed episode—my Italian connection, Padre Pio, stigmata, Rick L. Tucker with his graph of my relative clauses—into what I now see to have become the central strand of my life. For, sitting that evening in a hotel bedroom, the papers were all I had to read and I read the lot.

Coldharbour was a one-off. But the books that followed hadn't been bad either. There were things, mantic moments, certainties, if you like, whole episodes that had blazed, hurt, been suffered for—and they were wasted. I had written them, I saw, for nobody but myself, who had never reread them. The conference had operated in the light of certain beliefs. One was that you can understand wholeness by tearing it into separate pieces. Another was that there is nothing new. The question to be asked when reading one book is, what other books does it come from? I will not say that this was a blinding light—indeed, what are academics to do?—but I did see what an economical way there was for me to write my next book. I did it there and then, living by the shores of Lake Trasimene. I did not need to invent, to dive, suffer, endure that obscurely necessary anguish in the pursuit of the—unreadable. There, hanging in the fringes of the Apennines, my ex-chum's family history rendered invention irrelevant. So I wrote *The Birds of Prey* in next to no time, with no more than five per cent of myself—not the top five per cent either—sent it to my agent, together with some poste restante addresses, and drove off in a hire car.

Middle-age was leaving me and something more advanced was approaching and I didn't much like the look of it. Memory, for example. Now and then it was patchy where it used to be good. I forgot my ex-chum with great rapidity and the book, *The Birds of Prey*, even faster. My friends had become acquaintances. Since no one writes letters any more, they soon ceased to be even that.

So I drove. In what must have been about two years— I think two years, but I'm bad at dates and times and ages, my own included—I learnt the main road system of Europe and further afield than that. I learnt the high roads, motorways, the autoroutes, autostradas, autobahns, autoputs from Finland to Cadiz. In the days when it was still possible I drove the whole coast of North Africa and a bit of the west. But mostly it was Europe. I hired cars. Now and then, if I needed to write, I bought a typewriter. I kept a journal in longhand but found if I leafed through it the thing was terribly boring and made me feel faintly sick. But I always kept it even if only one sentence for a day. It was a compulsion, like having to avoid the cracks between paving stones. The relatively cheap but also efficient milieu of the motorway in every country, its spiritual emptiness, its pretence of shifting you to another place while all the time keeping you motionless on the same concrete waste—that kind of internationalism became my way of life, my homeland if you like. I never achieved the very young girl of the lustful imagination and hardly missed her. "Time, unnoticed, did its dusty work." There had been years when women had looked first then been told who I was. Now, on the rare occasions when I found myself socially among people, women were told who I was and looked afterwards. It was a curious repeat of or variation on the early years after my first book, *Coldharbour,* and before I met Liz. In those days I drove for two years in the States—Nabokov country, you might call it—selling my lectures on the academic merry-go-round. Later I drove in South America—well, never mind that. Now, however, it was Europe and extensions. I had a hobby, by the way, a hobby with no genesis, just like a book, the hunting of stained glass for no reason at all, just fun, nothing written down. I just like looking. I am in fact an authority on the stuff, though nobody knows so. I can date most glass to a decade, or at least defend my dating, though I've never tried. This eccentric enjoyment has turned me into something of a church fancier. You will have the darkest suspicions of me, what with Padre Pio and churches, but I have to make it plain that though I have spent many hours in, for example, Chartres cathedral, there is nothing religious about my interest in churches. It was art, the way of preventing light from entering a building when you don't want it there. Also churches are most often dark, cool places and ideal for recovering from a hangover. I suppose I ought to mention that I drank a lot now and then and at least more than "some" most of the time.

Stemming from *The Birds of Prey,* or at least from the film of it, I wrote some travel articles and a few short stories which are exercises in how to cheat the public. The stories were for the glossies. They relied almost entirely on the exoticism of the places where I collected news, money and mail from my postes restantes. They were descriptively brilliant, with the minimum of event and character, but all *garnished*, as the French might say, with national costume long after national costume had ceased to be found anywhere but at folk festivals. I had ceased when my Italian chum severed our connection to make an effort to be pleasant to women. I cultivated what you might call universal indifference. Sometimes the thought and feeling of life would merge into a wave of astonishment that made me exclaim silently inside myself, *this cannot be you!* But it was; and I now see that on the edge of sixty years old I had reduced myself to what would think least and feel least. I was eyes and appetite. I flew as an answer to any question. It was the motor roads all over again. If I wondered where I was going, I flew somewhere. If someone tried to arrange an interview, I flew away. If I had been too filthy drunk in one place, I flew to another. If the view from the bar or café became boring, why, someone had said something about the gorge of the Brahmaputra, so I would fly to Calcutta.

There was an odd fly in the ointment. You could call it a faint, a distant awareness of Liz: and I see now that I've written it down that it wasn't that at all.

It's difficult to explain. I never got over, never *have* got over, thinking I've seen her. I never did see her after I left England until I went back there. But I'd be sitting outside a café at one of those round, white tables that are as placeless as motor roads and I'd be watching a crocodile of tourists, all, it may be, following their guide down round the corner to the Uffizi, and when they'd gone I'd remember that—*surely!* It had been a gesture, a dress, a voice. I've even started to my feet and made a step to follow, then stopped because even if it were so, what was the point? I was once coming down the stairs from an osteopath in Brisbane and I stood aside to let a woman go up; then when she had gone into his office I turned to follow her until I remembered Capstone Bowers and I went away. I worried sometimes about all this, but then I found a solution to that bit of nonsense in my brain. I came across the account of a solo voyage round the world by some sensible man—sensible, I thought, because his voyage was so like mine, an attempt to avoid everything. He heard voices and the rigging began to say things to him that he only just couldn't understand. I "only just" didn't see Elizabeth in my deliberate, crowded isolation. Having my Italian chum about the place—or rather, my Italian chum having me about the place, one should say—had masked or prevented this curious series of non-meetings from happening. Now she was busily on her knees and I was alone. I thought time would cure me. Ha et cetera.

Yet here is a contradiction. My contacts were with waiters, chamber maids, receptionists, hostesses. I shared the occasional meal with some international commuter as rootless as myself. I remember one time, when only a little drunk, I and a man I never saw again argued as to which country we were in and agreed to differ. I forget who was right—neither perhaps. Then again, there was always bar talk. All the same, bit by bit it came over me. I was lonely.

How mixed all this is! But I had reached sixty that time when I flew into Zurich and I had drunk far too much on the plane. To put it mildly, I needed somewhere to recover and the airport doctor advised Schwillen on the Zurich lake.

Chapter III

So I made another of the predestined steps in my life.
Schwillen was inevitable and so was meeting them. It was
my first morning in Schwillen that it happened and I'd
drunk a little, not too much, and was feeling just about
right. I climbed a little bluff over the lake where there was a
monument to some Lithuanians. There was a park and a
castle and green-painted chairs to sit on. So I sat. I
remember contemplating with some pleasure the fun it
would be to have an aristocracy all named after cheeses
and contrariwise. *Le gratin* indeed! Then I became aware of
a large figure standing between me and the sun.

"Wilfred Barclay, sir? Wilf?"

"Good God."

"If I might—"

He was huge—really huge. Or perhaps I had shrunk.

"I can't stop you sitting down, can I?"

"It's really great to see you!"

"How are my dependent clauses?"

"I ought to explain, Wilf—"

"Don't bother. Go away and teach."

"Sabbatical, Wilf. Every seven years."

"So long? It seems only yesterday."

"Seven years, Wilf, sir."

"You served seven years for Leah. Her eyes will be
weak."

"No, sir. She's Mary Lou. I guess you don't know her.
There."

I looked where his eyes showed me. A girl was just
stepping on to the gravel patch where we were sitting.
She was very young, twenty, I thought. She had a pale

face and dark, cloudy hair. She was slim as a cigarette.

"Mary Lou, look who's here!"

"Mr Barclay?"

"Wilfred Barclay."

"Mary Lou Tucker."

Rick gazed down at her proudly and fondly.

"She's a real fan, Wilf."

"Oh, Mr Barclay—'

"Wilf, please. Rick, you lucky young devil!"

I shed forty years in a flash. Correction: I felt as if I had shed forty years. Rick was my friend. They were both my friends, this one in particular.

"Felicitations, Mary Lou!"

Somehow it was obvious they were just married, or if not "just", why, she looked like that, all grace and glow! I took her by the shoulders and kissed her. I don't know what she thought of the Swiss wine—Dôle—that I'd been drinking as early in the morning as that. I thrust her away, examined her from low, pale brow to delicate throat. Her cheeks had *mantled*. That was the only word and before you could repeat it her cheeks had paled and mantled all over again. Everything inside was at the surface in a flash; but then, it hadn't far to go.

"Late felicitations, Mary Lou. Husband and wife is one flesh, and since I can't kiss Rick—"

Tucker gave a yelp of laughter.

"—you take it out on Mary Lou! Hold it right there!'

A minute camera flicked into his right hand from his sleeve with the dazzling speed of a stiletto. The pic must be about in some drawer or other, perhaps in the library at Astrakhan, Nebraska. There'll be Mary Lou, her beauty dulled by the instant record, there'll be my scraggy yellow-white beard, yellow-white thatch and broken-toothed grin. The camera cannot have caught her warmth and softness. It was what you might call a close encounter of the second kind, no image of a girl but the pliant, perfumed, actual—I was not used to it and put very far off my guard. A wave of feeling pulsed up my right arm

30

from the thin covering over her waist. My ageing heart missed a beat and syncopated a few others. She was perfect as a hedge rose.

"Wilf, you and Mary Lou should have a beautiful relationship. After all she majored—"

Mary Lou broke in.

"Now, hon, we don't have to—"

But he was gazing down earnestly into my face.

"God, Wilf, Elizabeth is a dear person and I was truly sorry."

"Oh, Mr Barclay—"

"Wilf, please. Try saying 'Wilf'."

"I don't think I can!"

"Yes, do, do. Go on, just say it!"

"No, I, I can't—"

We were all laughing and talking at once. Rick threatened to beat her if she didn't, and I was saying I don't know what, and she was laughing beautifully and saying that, no, she couldn't, and—

"Oh, Mr Barclay, that quaint old house!"

Believe it or not, I never noticed. It was only later that I realized that my sometime quaint old house was where they had just come from. When we had done our silly laughter and paused, it was as if in expectation of some second act.

"Here. Why don't we sit down?"

There was a bench seat. I sat in the middle. Rick sat on my left, Mary Lou sat down somewhat gingerly on my right.

"Wilf," said Rick ponderously, "I have to ask a question."

"Not about books, for God's sake."

"No, no, but— Well, I suppose you're alone?"

"No constant companion. No just good friend. No seen constantly in the company of. D'you know, Mary Lou? I'm sixty!"

I paused, rather expecting Mary Lou to be surprised. After all, I was rather surprised myself. But she nodded solemnly.

"I know."

Rick leaned towards me.

"And you're writing, Wilf?"

A touch of the old irritation came back. I grunted. Rick nodded.

"That kind of trauma."

"Good God, man, it's years and years—unless you're talking about my . . . my Italian connection."

"All the same—"

"Complete change of life style. Fancy-free. Can make a pass at any girl in sight with no one to say me nay but the girl."

Mary Lou moved slightly along the bench. I had, after all, breathed in her face. I expect her mother had told her you can never be sure with men. Well. You can't.

Jake was laughing with a touch of the locker room.

"I'll bet they don't!"

"Wanna bet?"

"Not on my salary, Wilf. An assistant professor—"

"Assistant? But weren't you full?"

"Honestly, Wilf—"

"It may well be on your letter, somewhere in that quaint old house, nailed in a tea chest: '—of the Department of English and Allied Studies, University of Astrakhan, Nebraska'. I remember it so clearly because it led straight on to that night."

"Wilf. I'd sooner not."

His voice faded, as it had faded in Seville. Mary Lou was sitting very tall and looking straight ahead. She swallowed—a lovely movement of the throat, Eve's Apple. She spoke without turning her head.

"Remember, hon. Cross your heart."

"But, hon—"

"You best tell Mr Barclay, hon. You'll never rest quiet else."

"What is this, you two? Something I don't know about?"

"Mr Barclay. He wasn't a professor as of that date. He

was a postgraduate student and he borrowed the fare off'n his mom to come to you in vacation."

"I was desperate, Wilf. You were my, my—"

"Assignment?"

"Special subject. It's official, Wilf."

"Only remember, Mr Barclay, she was a really wicked person. Rick's told me about her."

"About who?"

"Ella. I'm glad you've told him you weren't a professor then, hon."

"I'm glad too, hon. So now I've told you, Wilf—"

"Mary Lou told me. Husband and wife—"

But Rick was staring across at Mary Lou with an expression of less than perfect devotion.

"—and I have tenure and I am an assistant professor and I have a kind of sabbatical."

"And I know you'll feel better now, hon. Now you can go on like you begun, hon. It's best. Always."

The sun was bright behind the trees, the leaves showering their shadows across the gravel. Every tiny wave sparkled on the lake. It all made me laugh.

"I'd quite forgotten what it's like to talk in—well, our mid-Atlantic lingo!"

I slid my arm along the back of the seat.

"So much for Rick's confession, Mary Lou. How about you? Anything to declare?"

"Well, no, I guess not."

She moved slightly away from me again.

"But you mustn't go!"

"It's not that, Wilf. She doesn't want to impose. She knows how generous you are. I've told her."

"That's right," I said out of my fatuity. "What's it to be, Mary Lou? The crown jewels or a moon rock?"

Mary Lou slid right off the end of the bench. It was deftly done for she rose to her feet, dusting off her calf-length skirt as she did so.

"I'll get back, hon. You two have so much to talk about."

She went very quickly and a cold wind poured down the

slope behind the bluff and dulled the lake to pewter. Somehow it brought the dustbin back to mind.

"Rick. You are a con man. Nothing but. My congratulations. It's far more interesting than scholarship."

"I was meaning to tell you, Wilf. I was going to be a professor. I knew that."

"Con men know they're going to be rich."

"But I *knew!*"

"Hell, what's a professor anyway? When I was young I thought a professor amounted to something. They're no better than writers. I eat 'em for breakfast. Taste different, that's all."

"Critics, Wilf! They make or break!"

"But what about John Crowe Ransom? From your letter I got the impression he was a real buddy. Did you tell *him* you were a professor?"

Rick's face went from scarlet to puce. Since I was looking sideways at him, I now saw from a new angle a curious bit of his individual body language. I'd seen it years before when he came to the house, bashfully determined to beard me in a lair rumoured to be dangerous. Later I'd seen it at that conference. I'd thought then it was some sort of illusion, I don't know why, that drawing back of the chin into the neck, that look up under lowered brows. But no. When embarrassed Rick really *did* draw back the bottom half of his face, project a forehead supposed to be, hoped to be, brazen and look up under his eyebrows like a crab from under a rock. He did it now and not even to me. It had become mechanical and he did it to the lake as if determined to be undaunted by that pewter sheet.

"Come on, Rick—out with it!"

"It began with a mistake by my—our—secretary in the office. Ella. I used to get letters addressed to Professor Tucker. It was the same for everybody, a sales pitch, flattery."

"So you took a leaf out of the commercial handbook. Bravo!"

"You'll never know what your work's meant to me."

"If anyone lets on what a con man you are, you'll be drummed out of the academic regiment."

"It was that goddammed girl. Me too, I have to say. I let it ride."

"You took a risk. Congratulations."

"Worth it, though. Her mistake earned me this, hopefully, intimacy, sitting here like this, side by side."

"How the hell else could we sit?"

"That girl, Wilf—" chin drawn back again, leaden waters fronted—"she liked me. She thought she was doing me a favour."

"And John Crowe Ransom?"

"I really forget, Wilf. I really do. We did meet."

Suddenly I saw that the waters were lifeless.

"What does it matter? I'm leaving tomorrow. Then Mary Lou'll be able to sit on this bench without falling off it."

There was a pause. Rick broke it.

"But you'll have dinner with us tonight?"

"All three of us?"

"Surely."

"Right. But you'll be my guests. Old man's privilege. The only one."

"Mary Lou's shy, Wilf. She always was. But she does know what a really warm person you are under that British exterior."

"And I thought I was international."

Rick stood up. He came out with one of his prepared statements.

"We've always thought of you, sir, as a really fine example of and credit to your Great Country."

He took himself off down the bluff after his wife. He left me there nodding solemnly like a porcelain mandarin and murmuring, *Be wary of Mary, don't be a prick with Rick.*

Then I added the loathsome words aloud.

"Hopefully in this encounter situation."

Quite quickly sanity returned to me. They had been to the "quaint old house". So this meeting was not accidental. They had wheedled my postes restantes out of Elizabeth, if not my agent. I was Rick's special subject. I was his raw material, the ore in his mine, his farm, his lobster pots.

But where was he getting the money to come in pursuit? Such things are expensive, as I knew from an early attempt to get some letters back.

I thought of this girl, Mary Lou, with the transparent face of that beauty which must surely be holy and wise. Not like the poor old padre!

"Born again perhaps."

The girl you meet every seven—no, every fourteen years, the one you meet, in fact, when it is all too late. I saw my sudden exhilaration for what it was, the symptom of my near-senility. I guessed how my breath must already stink of the morning's Dôle. There might be much in this for Rick. There might be something in it for Mary Lou, opportunity to admire with distaste someone whose books she had read. But there could be nothing in it for me but fixation, frustration, folly and grief. I determined to sear this tiny bud of the future before it was in leaf. Let them chase someone else. There were authors enough to go round after all, authors by the thousand; and all with foreheads of such brass or lives of such impenetrable rectitude they could afford the deadliest of all poisons about themselves, the simple truth. Whereas I—

Seated on the green-painted bench I endured a shower of pics out of my past. I leapt up and hurried back to the hotel. I murmured to the manager that I was in need of solitude. Smoothly he recommended the Weisswald, an apron of skiing country held up to the sun and now deserted in the off-season. I should stay at the hotel Felsenblick. The others were clean, of course, but that was all. I nodded and nodded and paid my bill, packed, filled in my forwarding address as the Hotel Bung Ho, Hongkong, and stole away.

There was a vast garage at the foot of the Weisswald and then a rock railway slanting up the hideously vertical side of the mountain. I kept my eyes shut all the way up. My fear of heights is pathological, which is perhaps why I am fascinated by them. More than that, I wanted to save the view of the high places until I got on level ground and could admire them without feeling the compulsion to jump. A porter led me, my eyes watching my feet, to the hotel. The manager had a suite, no less, at a reduced price and its balcony overhung the cliff. He threw open the door and ushered me through.

'See!''

One side of the sitting-room was french windows, with the balcony outside them. Beyond that was five miles of empty air. The manager threw open the french windows and invited me to come outside. I stood close to the glass. The balcony felt firm enough.

"It is the best," said the manager, "really the best."

Had I been able to walk forward three paces, I could have spat down two thousand feet, had I been able to spit.

"It is for you. A good place for a writer."

"Who told you I am a writer?"

"My brother, the manager of the Schiff. The suite and the view is for you. Cheaply."

I was being shepherded from one family business to another. I cast a nervous glance at the 00-gauge railway that was laid out for children half a mile below, then concentrated on the nearer pot plants. On the balcony there was that white-painted iron table I had sat at in the Schiff, four white-painted chairs and a white-painted *chaise-longue.*

"My car will be safe? It was unlocked."

"The car, sir?"

"The garage."

"Both will be safe, locked or unlocked."

There was a pause. The view was changing minute by minute. A white line divided a black cliff below a mile-high iced cake.

"What is that?"

"Where, sir?"

"There."

"The Spurli. It is a waterfall. At the moment, with little snow left, it is a thread. It comes from that valley up there where our army conducted manoeuvres—"

"Up there? Impossible!"

"To tell you the truth, I was there. I do so each year. I am a major. Then—a word of necessary advice. I should not try to walk for a day or two."

"You mean I should acclimatize?"

"That is the English usage, is it not? Our American guests say 'Acclimate'."

"But I've been in the Zurich area."

The manager made a dismissive gesture, as if the difference between Zurich and the English Channel was too small to be noticed.

"Nevertheless, you are not in your first youth, Mr Barclay, and a day or two of rest is advisable."

"I shall remember."

"And with our view before you, we shall hope to be the source, not to say the inspiration, of some notable creation, sir. This is the bell. Our pleasure is to serve you."

The manager bowed himself out. I moved forward a little. I did not look down over the railing—a gesture for heroes. I pulled the *chaise-longue* as far from the railings as possible, wrapped myself in a vast duvet from the bedroom, stretched myself out and contemplated the view. It continued to change, to reveal further fantasies of rock or snow. It revealed slopes where there had apparently been caverns, turned the black cliff that had been a backdrop to the Spurli first to grey then brown. I lay, inviting nature to astonish me. It did so, moderately, as usual. For the manager was wrong, of course. I had been in too many places, had seen too many extravagances. In any case, marvellous views don't get writers or painters going. They just give them an excuse for doing nothing. If anything, a marvellous view gets in a writer's way. It engages him to it. So I watched, as peaks appeared beyond what I had thought was there and a nearer one proved to be a white cloud. But we have seen the set pieces, the Himalayas, the Andes, the Sahara, storms at sea, cloudless, moonless nights unpolluted by the glow from cities, we have seen underwater fantasies and rain forests—ha et cetera. What a writer needs is a brick wall, rendered if possible, so that he can't see through it into a landscape suggested by the surface. I saw this would be another wasted week.

Nevertheless, thinking these thoughts and drinking more Dôle, I watched a bit of Switzerland for hours on end. Was I, I asked myself, a romantic after all? I did not think so. The thing led nowhere, the pleasure was an end in itself, brought forth no lofty or spiritual thoughts. It was the higher hedonism, a man becoming his own eyes. Late in the afternoon the Dôle and the hyperoxygenated air did their work and I fell asleep.

I awoke with the sun lowering itself round the westward limit of the balcony. My head seemed clear of Dôle despite the empty bottle. Was it the view? I played with the childish idea of adding a verse to Shelley's poem, this time celebrating the mountains as a cure for *gueule-de-bois*, like Chartres cathedral. With that thought my trancelike emptiness before Mother Nature filled with desire for a drink. I unwrapped from my duvet, visited the bathroom and went in search of the bar which was conveniently to hand. I wished to punish myself for the Dôle and ordered a hideous concoction of my own which contains, among other things, Alka-Seltzer and Fernet Branca. In appearance it resembles diarrhoea. Even the manager, doubling now as barman, was appalled. Nor did he understand my remark that I was punishing a bottle of Dôle but he accepted it and did as he was bid. I was flagellating my palate with my nasty drink, congratulating myself on my direct appreciation of natural beauty and celebrating my escape from the dangers of emotionalism into steady peace when a tall and massive figure stood at my shoulder.

Chapter IV

It was of course, as I should have expected, Assistant Professor Rick L. Tucker of the University of Astrakhan, Neb. He was rigged in outdoor costume, *Lederhosen*, long socks with dazzling tops and boots so thick in the sole they seemed to have brought lumps of pavement with them. His shirt was open at the neck under a pullover with the inscription OLE ASHCAN knitted into it. I thought for a moment he was being defiant about that dustbin he'd rummaged so many years ago—well, seven long years ago. But the inscription was no more than a winsome joke at the expense of the place where he was earning his lolly. The letters spread right across his chest, which was wide. The glow of mountain air about him, as expressed by his cheeks and the tip of his nose, made him seem wider and taller than ever. I had to look a long way up at him. When I turned to him with the first movement of indignation he drew his chin back only minimally.

"Hi, Wilf! I see you had the same idea as we did!"

"Don't be wet."

"Mary Lou, look who's here!"

I stared round the bar. Mary Lou smiled pallidly from the lap of a huge armchair in a dark corner.

"Hi, Mary Lou."

"Mr Barclay."

"Wilf."

She made no reply but looked withdrawn. I had that sudden feeling that all the preciousness of life had condensed itself—no, no, it must not be, could not be!

"Your juice, hon."

"I guess I don't even feel like juice, hon."

40

Rick turned back to me.

"Mary Lou is feeling the altitude."

"A girl for sea level."

I took my eyes away, deliberately.

"Hon?"

I looked back despite myself. Mary Lou had her hands over her mouth. Her large eyes became huge. She struggled to get out of the chair.

"Can't you see, you fool? She's going to throw up!"

Mary Lou threw up halfway between the chair and the door. Rick made a kind of triangular dash to the bar with glasses and to the door. Mary Lou disappeared through it. The manager looked dispassionately at the mess. He shouted through the open door at the back of the bar and, as if she had been waiting for the event, a fat, grey-haired woman emerged through it with mop and pail. Rick dutifully pursued Mary Lou to wherever their room was. I contemplated the sick with the detachment of a man who was drinking something even worse. I took my filthy mixture and wandered out of the hotel into the sunset. There were round metal tables (the same ones I always sit at) in the little square where one side was the hideous drop. I sat at the table I had sat at in, say, Florence, Paris, St Louis. Where was I? Moving, always moving. It was the manager of the hotel in Schwillen. I simply hadn't covered my tracks. Next time—

I got up, strolled a few yards up the path that led to the higher meadows and felt a deadly weakness. I was just able to reach my chair and table again. Time passed.

Rick was sitting by me and talking. I didn't know how long he had been there. He was sketching out the immediate future. There were said to be four splendid walks we could take. He would explore while I spent the day acclimating. He didn't need to acclimate, having been used to heights all his life. They said that one of the walks involved a little scrambling. I sat back in the chair, nodding at what he said and my chin hit my chest.

Mary Lou was coming down the path from the high,

41

flowery slopes. She was talking about solid geometry and explaining the three fundamental curves of the calculus by reference to the immense cone of mountain that stood over us.

Someone blew an alphorn, right there in the square.

"Wilf? Sir?"

I was the alphorn and blew myself again with another enormous honk.

"Asleep."

I blinked back into the sunset. The station was absorbing a procession of Swiss, German, Austrian walkers. They all seemed as wide as they were high. Rick was laughing.

"You said Mary Lou majored in math! Mary Lou!"

"Dreamed I was an alphorn. Pretty girl. Congratulations."

"She admires you."

"She like me?"

Pause.

"Hell, yes!"

"She play chess?"

"Hell, no!"

"Checkers?"

"You'll both be OK. By morning. By this evening."

"Dinner."

"Yeah," said Rick baldly, "we'd like to have you eat with us."

I felt ever so slightly embarrassed.

"This one's on me."

The three of us appeared to be the only people staying at the hotel, midweek and out of season. At dinner Mary Lou remained pale and ate next to nothing. But Rick talked for all three. The walk he'd explored had the damnedest views. Truly inspirational. Streams, trees, the treeline, flowers. After I had grasped that we were going to walk tomorrow I ceased to listen and endured my preoccupation with Mary Lou instead. She didn't seem much interested in what Rick was saying either. She stood up suddenly, so that oddly enough I got to her before Rick, who had been talking about the snowline. He took her from me and led her away. When he came back he apologized for her, which amused me all down one side of my face.

"She's enchanting, Rick. I thought it was a literary convention but, you know, when she feels faint she doesn't go green and ancient—she just goes even more transparent."

"She said she wouldn't go with us tomorrow."

"Doesn't she like anything? I mean—"

"You could say," said Rick carefully, "Mary Lou isn't physical."

"Cats? Dogs? Horses?"

He blushed, a slow burn.

"You were there, Rick, the two of you. Recently."

"It's a place where you lived for a long time, Wilf."

I thought of the place where I had lived for a long time. The only place. The quaint old house, the water meadows, trees, hedges, bare downs closing in the two sides of the wide valley, the huge oaks and clumps of elms that Elizabeth said were dying. I felt detached.

"Did you like it?"

"Hell, yes!"

"Why?"

I never thought to hear a grown man say it, but he did.

"It's so green. That white horse cut in the side of the hill—everything's so ancient—"

"When I was there last they had motocross up the hill on one side of the White Horse on Sundays. The university archaeological society was skinning the turf on the other."

"But the people, Wilf! The customs—"

"Incest, mostly."

"You're—"

"No, I'm not kidding. And don't forget the coven."

"You are, you are, yes you are, Wilf!"

"Usually reliable sources. Wilfred Barclay's Stratford-on-Avon."

"I don't think so, sir."

43

"What were you looking for? My finger prints?"

"I had to talk to her. There's a great deal only she knows."

"Well, I'm damned."

"And papers."

"Now look, Rick Tucker. Those papers are mine and nobody, *nobody*, is going to go mucking about with them."

"But—"

"It was a condition. The house is hers, then reverts to Emmy in the event of. The papers are mine."

"Of course, Wilf. She said it was all very civilized."

"Elizabeth? She said that? Why, it was—"

I stopped, not so much out of residual loyalty as caution. Elizabeth had been covering up, of course. It had been a rending, hateful match which would have broken my heart if I had had one and to which only Julian had managed to bring legal decency. I had given everything on my side, not out of generosity but just to be shot of the whole thing. Julian saved us from advertising the mutual hatred which linked us indissolubly for better or worse. Perhaps like me by now, she had worn away all but a vestige of the hatred and accepted the huge scar? Or had I? Had she?

"She said she had to keep them but they were nothing to do with her."

"My papers?"

"You've never understood, sir. You are part of the Great Pageant of English Literature."

He really did say that. It rolled forth like a statement being read out in court. *The accused wishes to state that he is part of the Great Pageant*—why, there was meat in it! *Prisoner at the bar, you have been accused of being, and with intent to deceive, a part of the Great Pageant*—

"Balls!"

Rick's chin was back, forehead thrust forward, eyes looking out from under his ledge of rock.

"So give over, professor."

"In any case, she refused me, Wilf."

"She never was promiscuous. I give her that."

"I know you're joking, sir. But I see the hurt."

"Well, for God's sake! How was Capstone Bowers?"

"Well, I guess."

"Good. Very good."

"She wouldn't even let me see the boxes."

"Good. Good."

"She said not without your permission. Written permission. That was the agreement, she said. 'Gentleman's agreement,' she said and laughed. You both laugh a lot. I'd like to research that."

"Vivisection. You don't know about my life. You aren't going to either."

A minute cup of coffee and a large brandy had appeared on my rush place mat. I warmed the brandy with cupped hands.

"It's important to me, Wilf. Very important. I'd give anything—*anything!* You don't know the competition— and I have a chance. There's a man—I'll tell you one day. But I must have your permission—"

"I said no, damn it!"

"Wait, wait! I'm not talking about the papers—there's time and maybe one day—but there's another thing."

"The devil of it is, I gave up drinking yesterday. Now here I am, without conscious volition, drinking brandy and really, you know, a little, just a little—"

"Another thing—"

"I'm what they call *just a little on circuit*. The condemned man ate a hearty breakfast. How odd it must be on circuit. Rather like motor roads. No one to talk to. Just booze and the papers of the next day's cases. Cheers."

"Wilf—"

I thought of judges and how little I knew about them. Lucky me. A long life of undiscovered crime. Those who didn't get away with it were exported to Australia. The criminals that stayed behind bred the likes of us. Take your pick.

I became aware that Rick had gone on talking. I interrupted him.

"I get drunk so easily nowadays. It's the altitude."

"Wilf, please!"

"Professor?"

"It means a whole lot to me. I can do no more than plead—"

"You wanna be a full professor? Emeritus?"

"Wilf. I want you to appoint me your official biographer."

Chapter V

I looked up at him and then a long way past him. My life, that life, that long and lengthening trail of—of what? Foot prints in the sands of. Snail trail. The evidence for the prosecution and, let us not forget, the evidence for the defence, if any, and the prisoner is not about to throw himself on the mercy of the court. Let him plead guilty, the social worker will come forward and testify in his behalf that he was kind to his old mum and horses, threw money about, often in the direction of his friends, had slipped many a bank note into this collecting box and that; all this, m'lud, I offer as a counterbalance to the prisoner's habit of scrawling lies on paper into a shape that the weak-minded have taken as guide, comforter and friend, allegedly, often to their cost. I would remind you, m'lud, that the principal witness for the prosecution, the man Plato, is a foreigner. Mr Smith, the case for the prosecution has been made. You will confine yourself to giving evidence as to the moral stature of the prisoner. Well, m'lud, if the truth is to be told he has been a real bastard. . . .

Those memories, how they sting, scald, burn!

At nineteen I was a bank clerk, allowed to take in savings, register cheques. I was supposed to be reading for banking exams in my spare time, ha et cetera, so that I might—who knows?—become a cashier and end up as a bank manager. I was just out of school—school for farmers' sons mostly, lads who couldn't pass the common entrance. Mum's shoestring riding stables sort of edged me in. She must have had some kind of pull, God knows what. So I could stand behind the counter with my old school tie well to the fore, smile brightly, as they used to say, while giving service without servility. The manager began by liking me because I could think of nothing better to do with my Wednesday and Saturday afternoons than play rugger. I was in a daze, I remember at the speed with which mum's death—she'd thought I might go into the Church because I liked reading so much—had projected me into this world of figures. Even the rugger club consisted of old men by my standards. After the game on Saturday there'd be mild high jinks in a pub somewhere. Christ, I was naive!

Almost the first game, or after it, there was a corner snigger—

"Where's young Wilf? He ought to try one!"

"One" was a pill. No, it wasn't a drug, as it might be today. It was a commonly advertised aphrodisiac. Well, at least I am able to offer some personal evidence in a sphere where the claims are contradictory and few men appear willing to put their own evidence on paper. The pill worked. Perhaps it contained a mite of Spanish fly. Perhaps it was a placebo. But it worked.

Yes, of course, they assured me, we'd all be going on to the girls, where else? So, watched carefully and roundly applauded, I took it—nineteen, just nineteen! Well. I told my ex-chum, did I not, that Padre Pio's stigmata must be nothing but suggestion? *Experientia docet stultos*, as Zonkers used to tell us when he gave us lines. I looked forward fearfully and libidinously. Of course, beyond the, shall we say, physiological plane nothing happened at all. The evening dwindled to half-pints drunk slowly, rugger songs, dirty talk and the odd remark tossed my way.

"Feeling all right, young Wilf? Sure? Ha ha."

As the hypnotist told me, God rot him, *You are very receptive to hypnotic suggestion, sir.*

Well, you wouldn't get such a thick-headed young fool today, they all know everything by the time they're ten. But I was left with the kind of erection so gorged it was a steady pain and on which masturbation had no effect whatever. All night I wrestled and moaned but there was

48

nothing for it. Next day I had to take my erection to the bank. All morning I stood behind the counter and my tie, smiling brightly at farmers, teachers, parsons, old ladies, young ladies bringing in the firm's takings for the week and taking out the pay for the employees. All day the knob of my cock wore itself raw against the waistband of my underpants.

"Maybe I can share the joke, Wilf."

He was examining me earnestly. Late light was fading from the window.

"Joke? How can it be a joke? I was thinking of my time as a banker."

"I never knew."

"Like T. S. Eliot."

The thought of T. S. Eliot and the ithyphallic bank clerk set me off again.

"I could give you a new slant on banking, Rick."

"Could you just mention the date for the record?"

"Sit still, man, and don't fuss."

It was the spirit of farce, of course. In one way I could describe my whole life as a movement from one moment of farce to another, farce on one plane or another, nature's comic, her clown with a red nose, ginger hair and trousers always falling down at precisely the wrong moment. Yes, right from the cradle. The first time I shot over a horse's head my fall was broken by a pile of dung. That's farce in a good humour, that is. It silvered into my mind, I remember, that if only *once* I'd come down on something hard, something not farcical—

Well. There was still time.

"Talk to me, Wilf."

Yes. He could have that. He could start with the pile of dung and go on to the bank clerk. I wouldn't mind, would even write it out myself, would go on telly and scandalize the box, if that was still possible. I found, to my surprise, that I could look back at the sturdy young man in a goodish suit, white shirt and school tie (a little too brilliant perhaps but all the simple colour combinations had been taken by

49

top places)—yes, I could look back at him with an amused toleration even an affection. I remembered—

"What *is* the joke, Wilf?"

—the time Wilfred Barclay was caught donating tuppence to the bank in order to square his figures; and the row with the cashier, since giving the bank small change was, in the cashier's view and in the manager's view and the bank's view and, for all I know, in the Bank of England's view, ethically worse than taking small change away from it.

The cashier was really passionate. He shoved my tuppence back at me.

"No one, no one at all, leaves this building until the accounts balance to the last penny!"

I was saved (or, as I would now say, my escape was delayed) by my rugger, which was approved of on every side. When I discovered Maupassant even rugger went. The end came. The end was a Scots bank inspector. I found myself quoting him to Rick.

"Ye know, Mr Barclay, ye've geeven me an entirely niew view of feegures."

The manager expressed his regret that a wing three of such brilliance should be lost to the bank and the town.

"But you see, Barclay, it's a question of heart. Your heart's not really with us, is it?"

That was when I had a spell as a groom, then went some way towards the stage. I carried a spear at Elstree and spent a few months as a provincial reporter, mostly writing up any point-to-point in reach. There was the war. When I came back with a few pounds, *Coldharbour* wrote itself—*I* didn't—Stein and Cowhorn published it, and hey presto.

A biography of Wilfred Barclay. Well, why not? Was the idea any more farcical than the material it would contain?

"And who is Lucinda?"

I came to with a start. It was the ageing man's failing of shortening the link between the words in his mind and the words on his tongue. Rick was regarding me intently. Of

50

course—he'd been there, shot by an air gun, the whole scene as deeply engraven in his memory as in mine. I shook my head and gave him what I hoped was an inscrutable smile. A shadow passed over the professor's face (as we say in our extravagant way) when he saw the shop was no longer open.

Lucinda was more of a problem, more mixed, more nearly on the grey edge of the impermissible. So much of it, though, if not all of it, was her idea, not mine. When it came to sex, Lucinda was a genius. If *she* chose to write her memoirs! Dear God, *Domine defende nos!* A book for none but the gallant investigators of the human farmyard. She was such an inventor! Folks, what you have been looking for, take it home with you, a present for the wife, the kiddies, the dear old folks in whose toothless caverns marge will not melt—something new!

It was the Jiffy camera—a sort of proto-Polaroid, I think. She had one before they were even on the market. She would, of course, she knew a man. Trust Lucinda! Even her car was a one-off job. But using the camera was her idea, and God knows why it was so exciting but it was and made you feel like the chap in 'The Eve of St Agnes', above a mortal man impassioned far, practically bank clerk standard, in fact. She was ten years older than me, preserved carefully and very nearly the last relic of the BUF. But to strip off the rectangle of film, then together, naked or half-naked in bed, to watch the faint shadows, shapes hardly filled with colour, which way up, and she'd cry, "There I am!" or "There you are!" Of course, she wanted faces, her own mostly and mine sometimes, but rarely on the same pic, not possibly on the same pic.

I know now that her compulsion to have her face photographed in such situations and only seconds later to see it again in full colour was a substitute for having it off at the crossroads and stopping the traffic; or like the empress who performed on stage with peas and a duck to roars, one must suppose, of Byzantine applause. One day she remarked casually that we'd better wait for a bit as she

51

thought she might have caught a dose of clap. I have never dodged so fast, even on the rugger field. After that—long after that—was the letter I'd torn up, together with photographs showing her and mostly anonymous bits of me, and thrown in the dustbin—fool!—only to have the resurrection man fish them out again. She kept the ones with my face on. Yet all that was *before* the days of Elizabeth—so why did memory of Lucinda in this most permissive age make me quiver so with unease?

Margaret. That was the connection. Directly I remembered, I twinged inside. I had done my best to forget the whole business with Margaret and succeeded pretty well. Only Lucinda was a part of it. I'd asked her advice. I'd told her about the mad, obscene letters I'd written Margaret, the only woman I'd wanted and couldn't have, the accusations, the curses on her marriage, oh impossible, vile—I must have been mad, literally mad. When I recovered I was desperate to get the letters back— mad all over again.

Lucinda was full of contempt.

"It's quite simple. The easiest thing in the world. You find a bent solicitor, give him her address and a hundred pounds. Go back after a month and he'll hand you your letters in a plain envelope. Nothing said. It's done every day. All finished, my dear little man. What a little man it is, den! God. I ought to charge you thousands for those pics."

"It would be—illegal."

"Criminal," she agreed cheerfully, "but that's the solicitor's affair. You're making a packet out of the film aren't you?"

"A small packet."

"If a man with money can't indulge himself with such services," said Lucinda with an air of calm reason, "what's money for?"

"I don't know a bent solicitor. Mine's so unbent he's rigid."

"There aren't any unbent solicitors. Only some less bent than others."

Sitting opposite Rick Tucker, who now had snow and stars behind him, it came over me in a breathtaking swirl of astonishment. More than thirty years before I had indeed gone by long and devious ways to a bent solicitor. I had given him money. I had made myself an accessory after the act for nothing, for less than nothing. When, standing in my flat by the fire that was intended to consume my own disgusting and pitiable letters, I opened the manila envelope I stood dumb for whole minutes. The letters were tied up with pink ribbon. I surfaced then from what must have been months of drunken misconception. They weren't my letters at all. They were her husband's, turgid, inarticulate offerings from that stupid house agent; but she loved him and they were preserved like relics. Mine—in a skyhigh pride I had never dreamed that anyone could destroy *my* letters (mad, mad, mad) but she had done just that—charitably too, since she could have turned them over to the law—she had burnt the obscene things as they came. Or worse—had she kept them indeed? Were they now afloat in the world, the wrong world? If so, their disappearance together with the disappearance of her husband's letters would be a clear lead, I was never free, should never be free from the surfacing of that possibility—

"I hope to God he broke the place up."

Someone was looking at me—staring.

"Wilf?"

I pulled my eyes away from his, allowed them to track down, his nose, a little broad, the bridge slightly sunken, his long upper lip, the lower one dropped a fraction from it. His napkin came into view, patted his mouth, disappeared again. He was wearing a shirt with white and brown stripes, very broad. We'd have thought them so vulgar when I was his age.

"Is anything wrong?"

I burnt her husband's letters, of course. I couldn't even send them back.

I lived in a state of dreadful sanity and apprehension. I

53

took off for South America as if the police were already after me. The thing surfaced for years, disguised in nightmares or strange half-waking dreams, until it had become a faint far-off thing only to be recalled when, as now, my mind was forced to walk backwards.

Odd to think that nothing would have happened without Lucinda. She was the sort of person who ends with hard drugs and charitable people saying she was her own worst enemy, hurting no one but herself. Little they knew or understood the adamantine chain that bound the lesser crime to the greater, led on to it step by step unless you turned and faced the fact instead of running from it. How wrong they would be about Lucinda! We are all members one of another. Ha et cetera.

"Can't I share the joke?"

"I suppose it's a joke. On a large scale. I'm drunk. Had too much brandy."

"Wilf, there's a strain of, call it diffidence, in you that won't allow you to see the interest in a biography—"

Amused by the bank clerk, ruefully, jeeringly accepting the follies of Lucinda's lover—(title for a romance in single syllables)—but the letters, Margaret, my crime—

"Just a note—and of course at this moment in time hopefully we should do no more than agree the parameters—"

Running. Always running, a wing three running in panic lest I should be grabbed by some enormous oaf from the scrum—

"Just a note, Wilf, signed by you and empowering me, particularly in the event of your passing on, I am after all a generation younger—"

Well. He *was* an enormous oaf from the scrum.

"Rick. You do me the honour of including me among kings, presidents, multiple murderers, telly personalities—"

He caught on in what for him was a flash.

"Also Thomas Wolfe, Hemingway, Hawthorne and—" here his voice sank in a kind of awe, "White Melville!"

"I'm not American. A defect, of course. However, Elizabeth used to say—"

"Yes, Wilf? Go on!"

Her nastiest thrust; because like all deeply wounding marital broadsides there was a truth in it that only she could know. She told me (sitting the other side of the scrubbed kitchen table, all very homey), she told me that given half a chance I would act the genius, the great man—

That's what you always wanted, Wilf—God, don't I know it?—particularly before any pretty girl who's fool enough to come near you and take you at your own valuation, the sacré monster outside the accepted rules, a national treasure, the point about you being words that the world would not willingly let die whereas what you write is—

"Popular."

"It's a common misconception, Wilf."

"That my work's popular?"

"Hell, no. I mean that what's popular is—"

"—inferior."

"I didn't mean— I wanted her side of the story."

Her jeer had been the work of a scalpel. It was one of the many things that had kept me running, that made me shun that offer and that more and more made me hide myself away, because apart from other considerations it proved to—to whom? her? me?—that I sought no fame, struck no attitudes.

"What did you mean by 'her side of the story'?"

"I understood, Wilf, sir. The need for freedom. Why even with Mary Lou, between you and me—"

"Her side of the story."

"She was real nasty about some time you, like she said, 'shot off' to South America. She was having trouble with Emily. I forget which country in South America. When would that be?"

It was strange. I was seeing a process. It was not an intellectual concept, it was felt as well as seen, feared as well as grasped. It was simple, trite. It was universal. It was just one thing coming out of another—oh, just that, no more—Margaret, the letters, Lucinda, my fright, my running and running, one thing after another—

South America.

What year indeed? What would he turn up, dull and indefatigable, treading through my past life with his huge feet, shoving his nose down to that old, cold trail? A really modern biography without the subject's consent. Cheap printing in Singapore, ten million pulp copies from a backstreet factory in Macao. No control, sold over or under every counter. How they would laugh at Wilf Barclay, masturbating round South America in sheer fright of police and fear of women. Barclay got his fear of the clap from way down by his feet and Lucinda's idea that a night on the town was for her to be had against the dockyard wall by a dockie and, if possible, by the dockie's mate. And Barclay's heroic encounter with a revolution—three days spent shivering in a cellar; and so driving in a panic towards safety! He would turn it up.

Dead.

How closely would they look? How worthy was I of being dug round? Worth it to Rick, evidently, who could find no one better, no one behind whom the pseudo-scholars were not queueing up in our dreadful explosion of reconstituted rubbish. He would have access to more mechanisms than Boswell, not just paper, not just tapes, videos, discs, crystals with their hideous, merciless memories, but others, sniffers, squinters, reconstitutors, mechanisms doubtless that listened in a room and heard echoes of every word, saw shadows of every image that were trapped on the walls, like Capstone Bowers's gun.

Dead.

Of course. In South America, never mind where, even now there would be a record. That Indian—or perhaps not. It was so dark and I only had sidelights because of getting away and my determination was to say if necessary that he walked right across the road into my headlights—Was there any way in which they could find out that in panicky forgetfulness I had been driving along that dirt

56

road as in England, on the left-hand side? They say if you stop, the other Indians will kill you. It was an occasion to be pushed back down and down and away and at last hardly believed in, *not* believed in, though never forgotten. It was near-enough jungle, and anyway it was an Indian, probably and quite possibly he wasn't killed or even injured much, might have been an animal. Then I'd driven fast through a ford so that water had cascaded clean over the roof. Who could examine that river for bloodstains? Will all the waters, ha et cetera, and unlike her I didn't really *know* anything. Nudged a shadow and the slight shock, the rutted road, the cry, a bird or something. If there was a record—such and such an Indian found, well, dead—I'd told no one, not even myself, only gone over it later, over and over— How could I have gone back after ploughing through the ford? Go back again? Put myself in the hands of some louts in uniform and all to explain that I *might* have, wasn't sure—the language was the difficulty, of course. My Spanish wouldn't be up to it. I'd end by accusing myself through sheer inability to cope with the subjunctive.

Hit and run.

Happens every day somewhere, probably with extenuating circumstances, as in this case, clearly.

"—so, believe me, she did full justice to your genius."

I surfaced from molten metal.

"Genius?"

"That's what she meant."

"Nonsense. Don't forget I know Liz—oh I know her! She thought I had talent, ingenuity. I hit the jackpot. Someone has to."

Oh God, oh God, oh God, the process, link by link, we don't know what will come from this seed, what ghastly foliage and flowers, yet come it does, presenting us with more and more seeds, millions, until the whole of *now*, the universal Now, is nothing but irremediable result.

"If you could only see your way."

"That's funny. That's very, very funny."

57

"Just your signature with a sentence or two appointing me your literary executor, no harm, I'd co-operate, of course."

"I'm a bit drunk. Talk tomorrow."

"And, you see, I should be authorized to catalogue the papers left in her charge."

I contemplated his eager, diffident, stubborn face, that of the prospector who had chipped quartz and seen the yellow gleam inside it. My sentence and signature would confirm his staked-out claim. Then the letters, manuscripts, journals, journals right back to school days—

Jeffers is a frightfully good chap and I am keen on being his— it's marvellous being in the second with him—Jeffers caught a frightfully good catch off my bowling at first slip—I told him it was a frightfully good catch and he didn't seem to mind my speaking to him— Thank God that kind of farcically misplaced emotion had never pursued me into adulthood to make an even deeper confusion of life!

He was continuing to stare at me.

"So if you could see your way—"

"I've seen it, the whole lot, inch by inch."

There was no doubt of it. Given the least slackening of attention on my part, Rick's face, or his two faces, would slide apart. Well, why not? He had two faces.

"Of course, Wilf, where you wanted it would remain in confidence."

With considerable effort I brought his two faces together. I had an idiotic thought that he probably kept a different expression in each face, which was why when you merged them they cancelled each other out.

"How the devil did I get like this? Haven't drunk much."

"It's the altitude."

"Used to be the lobster. You know. Thingummy."

"Pickwick."

"Age and decay. No, Rick, duty and dereliction leads me back to solitude."

"Shelley."

I had to respect that, however unwillingly, because I only knew the quotation by a freakish chance. The line was in Shelley's scraps, not his published works. How the devil? Since my time they'd have published it all, of course, a Shelley factory like the Boswell factory, leave no leaf unturned, never mind what the poor bugger thought about it himself. Death pays all debts. Christ!

"Proper parlour game, isn't it?"

"Look, Wilf, I could write the whole thing out on this menu. The manager could witness it, you could sign it, then the whole thing would be done."

"Signed and sealed. We could seal it with the bottom of a brandy glass. S.W.A.L.K. No, that's different."

"I'm not following you, sir."

"Ha! Something you don't know! Victory!"

"I'll write on this one. 'I hereby authorize Professor Rick L. Tucker of the University of Astrakhan, Nebraska—'"

"Getting both feet in the door, aren't you?"

"There you are, Wilf. Use my pen."

Rick's balloon glass still had much brandy in it. I took it, spilled some on the back of the menu. I pressed the foot of the glass into the mess. It left some sort of circle like a seal.

"You needn't write where the brandy is, Wilf. Write there, on the side where the menu's dry."

The whole truth and nothing but the truth. Not even the time plant with its clouds of seed but other plants of this and that, all busily flourishing in the present and pressing on into my future—deeds unknown, but to be resurrected—

"No, Rick, no! I'd rather die than say yes!"

"Wilf—*please!* You don't know what it would mean to me!"

"Oh yes I do indeed. And what it would mean to me."

I printed a large, fierce NO on the back of the menu and held it out to him.

"A memento of a happy occasion."

Chapter VI

This isn't going to be an account of my travels. I suppose it's mainly about me and the Tuckers, man and wife. It's about more than that, though I can't really say what, the words are too weak, even mine; and God knows, by now they ought to be about as strong as most words can be.

Cry, cry.

What shall I cry?

Useless to cry. We have no common language. Oh yes, there is language all right, as for example regulations for transporting flammable materials by air or how to make your own Russian salad. But our words have been clipped like gold coins, adulterated and struck with a worn stamp.

Well there.

I put myself to bed and did not get up next morning. As the manager had said, I needed to acclimatize. Rick came and knocked so insistently that I had to let him in, even though I'd only just got round to drinking my breakfast coffee. He said Mary Lou was having her breakfast in bed too. He commented on my sitting-room, said what a marvel the view was. Their window looked out on the back of a chalet so near you could count the flies on it.

"Mary Lou is welcome to my view any time she feels like it."

Rick paused, then said they might take me up on that. Was there anything he could do for me? For example, did I need anything done about the hire car? He looked covetously at the journal open on my bedside table. I shut it pointedly. Rick asked if I had anything to dictate. His machine—

"Nothing. For God's sake, what do you think I am? A writer?"

He was electing himself my secretary.

"Goodbye, Rick. Don't let me keep you."

He ignored this and said he'd spend the day exploring the way along to the Hochalpenblick.

"Then we can go again tomorrow, if it's not too much for you."

"When Mary Lou is strong enough."

He thought about that remark for a while. I amplified.

"When the going gets too tough she can give you a hand dragging me along."

"She's happy to sit, Wilf."

"Not a sports girl?"

"She just loves your Wimbledon."

"Preserve us."

"I'll tell her you said to look in later."

"Did I?"

"The view, Wilf, the view!"

"Ah yes. The view. Mary Lou and me, we'll sit side by side and admire the view. She'd better not fall off the balcony."

"I suppose it's no good asking—"

"Not the slightest."

Rick thought for a while.

"Still," he said at last, "I'll ask her to bring it."

He went away, still nodding to himself. I forgot him, dressed and sat looking at the view. After all, it was what the hotel was supposed to be for. I have just examined what remains of my journal for that year—one of those journals so soon to perish in the holocaust—and find the date unusually full. There's nothing about the view but much about the glamour of young women, Nimue and the Shakespearian mirages, Perdita, Miranda. There's an attempt at describing Mary Lou but it is scribbled out and the Wilfred Barclay of that date writes about Helen of Troy! He comments on the way in which Homer gets his story across by describing not the woman but her effect on others. The old men on the wall watch her pass and say it is small wonder such a woman caused so much trouble, nevertheless let her go home before we have even more trouble! Or some such words. I've only read Homer in translations but that's what I remember. Well. Mary Lou made the sun come out on the lake and when she went the sun went with her. Mary Lou threw up and one was instantly sorry for her transparent face instead of being— as if Wilf did it, for example—disgusted. I can't—I couldn't—even describe her hands, so pale and slim and small. I ended, I find, by comparing myself to the old men on the wall. Yes, let Helen go home before there's trouble.

I had written all that I remember, despite the view, when there was a knock at the outer door. I crossed the lobby and opened it to our little Helen, who held a tray with coffee for two on it.

"Come in! Come in! Here—let me take that—do sit down!"

I was in a state of absurd confusion. Mary Lou folded herself into a chair and destroyed any attempt I might have made at direct description before I got it on paper. She rested her hands in her lap, wrapped her ankles round each other as in deportment. She turned her head to gaze out of the window and it seemed that localized movement altered every line of her body.

"You have a truly wonderful view here, Mr Barclay."

"Wilf, please, as before. Yes, I'm finding it difficult to look at anything else."

Defeated by holiness, the medieval illuminators stood their saints in a world of gold; then later, as perhaps— vision—became more selective, set a saintly head against an aureole. Beauty too, I think; which was what the old men saw as they sat on the wall, their voices thin and dry as the stridulation of crickets.

"Truly inspirational."

"My God, yes. There aren't any words."

"Reminds me." She unzipped her little handbag. Put back her hair with the flow of one forearm then took out an envelope. "Rick said to give you this."

"What is it?"

There was a change of colour in her face, very slight—but then everything about her seemed suggestion rather than fact. Perhaps she didn't exist at all but was a phantom of absolute beauty like the false Helen who caused all that pain to seek her through the world.

"Rick said to give it you."

"May I?"

There was another smaller envelope inside it, which had a note wrapped round, *Gone prospecting for our walk tomorrow. Hope Mary Lou has more luck than I did. Rick.*

I glanced at Mary Lou, who had her head turned away. She was looking at the view, of course, her hands grasping the arms of her chair not quite gracefully. I opened the inner envelope. It contained a sheet of hotel stationery with a sentence or two typed on it, appointing Assistant Professor Rick L. Tucker of the University of Astrakhan, Nebraska, as literary executor and giving him such access as he might require to the papers currently in the care of Mrs Elizabeth Capstone Bowers. My name was typed at the bottom with a space above it for my signature.

I looked at Mary Lou again.

"You don't know what this is?"

She answered in what can only be called a tiny voice.

"Rick said to give it you."

Avoiding the lie direct, poor girl. It might be so. Probably she loathed me and the whole situation. It was an unfair loathing, for I *had* tried to get away and been followed to the Weisswald.

"Tell me, Mary Lou. What do you want for Rick?"

Mary Lou thought; or rather, she tried to think. The effort produced a slight corrugation in her lovely forehead, no more.

"Oh come! You must have some idea!"

"Whatever he wants, I guess."

"Full professor? A chair? Books? Television appearances? Fame? Wealth? Maybe something in or from—I don't know how these things work—the Library of Congress?"

"I—"

"Yes?"

"Wouldn't you like some coffee, Mr Barclay? Cream? Sugar?"

"Just black. Wilf, please. Look, I'll put it another way. Have you any idea at all why Rick latched on to me? You see, writers are ten a penny. A hundred a penny. There are probably more writers than there are professors, seeing that some of each are also the other. Come, no flattery. I want the cold, honest truth."

"I guess he admires your work."

I bowed. But Mary Lou went on with much simplicity.

"I expect I shall too."

It took me some time and most of my coffee to find an answer to that one.

"Indeed, my dear, they are very adult reading—except *The Birds of Prey*, of course. I rather let myself down with that one. *Condottieri!*"

She nodded sagely.

"That's what Rick says."

"Oh he does, does he?"

"Yes, sir. He said like as not you wrote it with the film in view."

"I did not! Only, only—you know, people were like that in the fourteenth century. It was quite natural to— swashbuckle. In Italy anyway. Well. So. If he thinks like that, why is he stuck with me?"

"He said no one else was doing you as of this moment in time."

"I'm wounded."

"He couldn't find anyone. He did look, Mr Barclay, Wilf, because I did too. I was his student, you know. We worked together on you, sir. He said in that kind of study you can be beaten by a nose. He said it was essential to be quick as well as exact. We had to know the subject thoroughly."

"Me, in fact."

"He said he was investing our time and money in you—

Wilf—and we couldn't afford to make a mistake."

"Maybe he made a big one."

"It *was* the back room on the first floor, wasn't it?"

"I don't know what you're talking about."

"Felstead Regina."

"The cottages? The one at the end of the lane? Looking out into the woods?"

"Yes, sir, where you were born. We got photographs. That was the room, wasn't it?"

"So my mother said. She ought to know. My God."

"It was a small window."

"My God. My God."

"The man who lives there now didn't mind at all. He let us go up."

"You haven't got a photograph of the house where I died?"

"Sir?"

"My God."

"Have I said anything—?"

I poured myself more coffee and drank it in one gulp.

"No, no. Please go on. You are—you are helping Rick."

"Well. There's Mr Halliday, you see."

"I don't know a Mr Halliday."

"He's rich. Real rich I mean. He's read your books. He likes them."

"It's nice when rich men can read."

"Yes. It's nice for them, isn't it? He liked your second book best, that's *All We Like Sheep*."

"How do you know the names of my books when you haven't read them?"

"I majored in flower arranging and bibliography. His secretary, that's Mr Halliday's secretary, she said he particularly liked *All We Like Sheep*. She said he had noted one sentence particularly."

"Ah."

"Let me see if I can get this right. It was where you admit to liking sex but having no capacity for love."

After that neither of us said anything for a long time.

How long? In a novel I'd watch a clock on the wall, perhaps noting the ornamentation round the glass, and then be surprised to see how the minute hand had moved from ten to upright. There wasn't a clock on the wall. Well. I'd think thoughts. But there wasn't anything but a long time.

Mary Lou put down her cup.

"Well—"

"No—not for a minute. Don't go. I mean, why? Why Mr Halliday? Is he advancing lovelessness as a programme? For God's sake!"

"No, Wilf. Mr Halliday is very fond of ladies."

"Then I don't see where I come in. Let's leave the question. He probably picked me out of a reference book with a pin."

"He did not, now! He read that book—"

"*All We Like Sheep.*"

"—and then he ordered all the others—"

"Majestic!"

"—then he sent his secretary to ask round. She asked the President of Astrakhan. You see Mr Halliday had already given them the ecumenical temple, the skijump and the snow machine and the courts for real tennis—"

"I quite see he had a pull. He interviewed Rick—"

"Like I said, Mr Barclay, it was his secretary. He avoids all human contact. At least—"

"Except for his collection of women. The old devil!"

"But he's not old, Mr Barclay. Why, he's no older than you are!"

Pause.

"He hasn't written best-selling novels by any chance?"

"I don't think so. No. I know so. But you can see it was a real break. I mean after Rick had done phonetics he decided to specialize in you—because he did like your books, Mr Barclay, he really did. Then Mr Halliday's secretary communicated with the President of Astrakhan who asked Professor Saunders and there you are!"

"But a man as rich as that could afford more than one author—he could collect them like ladies!"

Mary Lou nodded. Then just when I thought my humiliation was complete she gave me a short list of other writers in whom Mr Halliday was interested. I had never read any of them.

I picked up Rick's letter, looked at it then set it down again. Men without love. There was something in it. Mum, the father I never knew, Elizabeth, Emily. Admittedly the man in *All We Like Sheep* who had claimed to have no capacity for love was nothing but a character I had sketched in for plot purposes; but did he, after all, speak for me? I was sometimes lonely. But that was the loneliness of a man who wanted *people about*, the noise and shapes of people, a certain liveliness. I desired with lessening frequency the shape of a female body to use. Even this recognition of the exquisiteness of Mary Lou's femininity was not in any way, I told myself, crude—it was partly paternal, protective, compassionate, sad.

She got to her feet.

"Well."

"Must you go?"

I could have done something harmless and explanatory like taking her hand and kissing it. I could have used my rhetoric. Men without love! All this danger in less than twenty-four hours!

But she was guessing that yes, she must go and she was thanking me for the coffee, both of us having forgotten that she had brought it with her. After I had closed the door behind her I stood in the little lobby, staring at my empty cases where they lay on the appropriate stand. It was useless and fatuous. I must get away, now, not just from him but from her as well. To be *limed* by five feet a few inches of child, to be limed by nothing but a young body that supported a mind about as interesting as a piece of string!

For if that mind supported the body, the body would have been—awful.

No. I was unfair. She did not like lying, tried not to. She tried to steer a course between what she knew Rick wanted and what she knew was right—she was a moral being and who was I to be critical of that? She did not like me. Who was I to be critical of that? She had not read the great works of Wilfred Barclay. Well. There were others, after all. Oh, she was still in the trance of marriage! She was still full of secret delight in what she knew and nobody else had ever known, the feminine delight of giving, of knowing yourself a possession, a chattel, and knowing you must keep that a secret from your man in the very moment that you delight in it, let him believe you play at what you know is the core of all human life. That dullness of mind, slowness of reaction, which I had interpreted as the measure of her intellect might be no more than her indifference to a man three times as old as she was but to whom for her husband's sake she must remain, at all costs, polite.

It was time I had a sleep before the rigours of eating dinner. I undressed and lay down. The old men chirred like grasshoppers on the city wall as they watched the girl go by. Small wonder that such a girl should be at the heart of so much trouble and sorrow. Small wonder young men should be willing to risk so much for her love. Nevertheless, let her go back to her own country before she is the cause of death to more young men. Old men. Old clowns, old bastards.

Chapter VII

I dreamed a lot which is supposed to be healthy, but I remembered my dreams which healthy or not is unusual with me. Elizabeth used to say I had no unconscious mind but that everything was accessible. In her world that meant I was like a stall with nothing but knick-knacks for sale and shoddy. Why did we ever meet? A Hindu doctor I used to know said we should continue to meet until we learnt but he never said what.

My dreams were about femininity *tout court*. I also dreamed myself out of bed and through the french windows on to the balcony. I dreamed myself watching the great glacier on the other side of the valley; and under some confused memory of what Elizabeth had said, I saw that it was my own consciousness that hung there. I understood what a wearisome business it was, this dancing awareness, this glitter of the mind from which I constructed my implausible but amusing stories. But then I dreamed myself into a state of worry because the balcony was revolving outwards and would tip me off at a certain angle; so whether unconscious or conscious, my dreaming mind flipped and I knew I was one of a series of butterflies that Mr Halliday had pinned into a showcase though the pin didn't hurt and I couldn't read the Latin name written under me. So I woke up with an uneasy feeling that I'd done a very poor prose and old Zonkers would be mifty! There was what the psychological boys (and the theological boys) call considerable *affect* left over from the dreams. That is to say, I woke up in a lather of sweat and was very glad to be sixty years old and in the Weisswald. The happiest days, ha et cetera.

Some "sacré monster", as Liz would have called me.

I showered and by that time it was too late for tea and not too early for the bar. I dressed quickly and went there. Through the window I could see a file of Austrian, German, Swiss walkers going the *other* way, that is, back to the rack railway; all short and wider than they were long, with sweat patches on their *Lederhosen* and feathers in their hats, and all giving an impression of a set of figures going to be put back in their box. I had settled at the bar while the manager was making my vile concoction for me with his deliberate absence of distaste when Professor Tucker erupted through the door.

"Hi, Wilf, you old stick-in-the-mud!"

"Hi yourself," I said, with a sour feeling, "assistant professor."

"I've seen nothing like it, even where I come from!"

"Sorry, but I do not intend to scramble."

"You don't have to. There's a handrail for miles. How was it with Mary Lou?"

"She mentioned Halliday."

That stopped him. After a bit he decided to laugh. You could see the process of decision. He was like one of those bits of engineering history, a Victorian pump, constructed with immense labour, skill, dedication, all green paint, oiled steel, steam—and turning round as slowly as a planet.

"A real character, Mr Halliday."

"Unreal."

"I was going to tell you about him."

"Natch, as you used to say."

"You'll eat with us?"

It was common sense not to be under the slightest obligation.

"You must both dine with me. No, I insist. It's my pleasure."

"Do you mean that?"

"Does anyone?"

Rick breezed away—a little more thoughtful perhaps but

70

still breezing. I considered a memory of his face. A day's mountain sunlight had turned his nose, cheeks and forehead to apples, cherries, tomatoes. I shifted my head this way and that until I could catch a glimpse of my own face between the contorted bottles in the inevitable mirror at the back of the bar. I couldn't qualify for the description of "red-faced Englishman". I looked more like some kind of leather that had been stowed in an attic for generations and was dusty and cracked. Dimmish eyes looked back at me and there were the tiny red worms of veins here and there in my nose. Nobody knew that face, I thought. A writer isn't like an actor or musician. His face isn't his fortune. It's his misfortune and then again perhaps not. It's his anonymity. If I wanted real fame, i.e. recognition in the street, I should wear a hat with "Author of *Coldharbour*" stuck in the front of it. I was happy not to want fame and thus give Elizabeth the lie.

I was already in the little restaurant when Rick and Mary Lou came in. He and I were wearing casuals but Mary Lou, I was obscurely worried to see, had made a real effort. She had a lot of bouncing, fluffy skirt but above the skirt the dress followed her delicate lines closely and ceased to exist as low down as Swiss *moeurs* permitted. For tourists that is very low down. It crossed my mind that if she had been trying, she couldn't have chosen a dress more calculatedly "with the older man in mind". However I seated her, deftly inserting her chair under the skirt—my parlour trick—and had had my own inserted by the manager when the whole place exploded.

"Dammit, man, who said you could take a pic?"

"Now, Wilf, just for the record—"

"There isn't going to be any record."

"You should have asked, hon."

"I didn't think Wilf would mind, hon."

"Rick."

"Yes, Wilf?"

"Don't do it again, hon, ever. I'll sue."

The manager had disappeared—hotelier's tact. We

inspected our menus and I passed the time boring them with a description of meals that I'd had in one place or another. The open air made Rick excited and voluble, once a little drink had helped him. Mary Lou was more silent and seemed worried, I thought, as if expecting Rick to make a fool of himself. Then just when I had tried and failed to raise a smile on that exquisite young face she changed her mind about not drinking. She said she'd like a large vodka, please, which Rick acclaimed as if she'd won a prize of some sort. Then as if I were the only person to be bored by my recital I found them both animated and myself dull, moodily jealous of their youth and wondering what the devil I'd got myself into. Rick talked about astronomy—apparently there was an observatory somewhere in sight—and bewailed the fact that they could see so little Swiss sky from their window. Mary Lou looked absent. Rick turned to her from me.

"Was there any sun, hon?"

"Sun, hon?"

"In our room this afternoon, hon."

"Why none, hon, I guess not."

"If you want sun or stars," I said, "there's always my balcony. Let's adjourn and have a look. What's it like outside? We might even—"

Rick stood up promptly. Mary Lou seized her hand bag and fled.

"What does she call it, Rick? The powder room? I collected them in the States: kings and queens, dukes and duchesses, guys and dolls, chiefs and squaws—that one was interesting, don't you think? Sociologically, I mean. It should have been braves and squaws. But then, that was all years ago. Perhaps now—but the custom's spreading. I've even seen it in England. Cultural imperialism."

"We'll be happy to see your stars, Wilf."

"What promotion. Have another drink before—it's the butt end of the bottle."

Rick sniggered. I said no more and we waited, standing, while he beat his fingers restlessly on the table.

72

"You know, Rick, two bottles between three is a sign of incipient alcoholism. Since Mary Lou drank nothing but that vodka—does she know anything about astronomy?"

There was a long pause. Rick came to with a start.

"Sorry, Wilf, I didn't—"

"Mary Lou. Astronomy."

"She's interested."

"I'm not, you know. Oh yes I am. Damn the wine. Waiter!"

It was the manager, of course. I asked him for a bottle of brandy, which he brought after a time. Rick continued to drum with his fingers.

"For God's sake, man—haven't you had *enough* exercise?"

"I don't get it, Wilf."

He knocked back his brandy out of the balloon in a way that was positively contemptible. I played the civilized game, warming the balloon with my hands, breathing in what I supposed was the aroma, though I have practically no sense of smell at all. Time passed.

Mary Lou came back from the powder room paler than she went. Perhaps she had thrown up again. Rick held another shot of brandy in his balloon.

"Wilf would really like us to see his stars, hon."

Mary Lou gave a little gasp.

"That would be fun, hon."

"The freedom of the balcony, my dears. No charge."

I picked up the brandy bottle. Rick stopped in his stride towards the door.

"Got to go to the john. You two go right ahead."

I went on with the bottle, got the door open for Mary Lou, conducted her through the little lobby, across the sitting-room where Rick's paper still lay on the table. I opened the french windows and she walked straight through, frou, frou, out on to the balcony.

"Careful!"

She was right by the railings. She put her hands on them on either side of her, leaned out and looked down.

73

"For God's sake! Sorry, my dear—I've got a thing about heights and oddly enough for other people more than myself. I can just about stand nearer a cliff than I can bear to see other people doing—standing—looking down, I mean. I just don't like heights anyway. Silly old me!"

Obediently as a little girl, she straightened up, took a pace, two paces back. I went to the switches.

"I'll turn the lights off."

A sky loaded with stars came in close enough to be touched.

"What sparklers, eh? A girl's best friend."

I stood by her shoulder, wondering why it was that I who could not detect the aroma of brandy could nevertheless detect the trace of perfume in her hair. I came even closer.

"Mr Barclay—"

"That's formal all of a sudden."

"Rick is desperate. He really is!"

"Why are we talking about Rick?"

It was a corny line, worthy of Dei Caitani in *The Birds of Prey*. In fact they used it in the film—tongue in cheek, of course. My arm came up, seemingly of its own accord, gave her further shoulder a little pat and rested there on the naked skin. My heart lurched then beat like a drum. I could hear my blood in my ears.

Mary Lou did nothing. Less than nothing. It was curious, impossible. (Mary Lou is not physical.) Perhaps it was on the edge of extrasensory perception. Perhaps it was on the verge of spiritual experience. After all, they must come in every shape and size according to the climate, must they not? What I felt was submission, an unnatural stillness, a kind of weight. Her—or perhaps I should say the—shoulder seemed less alive than marble. Somehow marble would have felt—would have felt— would have— *This* naked shoulder was less human than a doll's, was like the shoulder of some angled and impossible model in a shop window, plastic fashion, no more. She seemed to grow heavier by the moment, wholly passive.

Right from the soles of my feet, through the drink and the vague, libidinous fantasy of ageing, there swelled feelings that overwhelmed everything else—humiliation and sheer, unalloyed rage. To know myself accepted, endured not even as in honest whoredom, for money, but for *paper*!

So we stood side by side before the stars with nothing to do, nothing to say. We were so still an onlooker might well have thought us starstruck.

At last I took my heavy hand away from her heavy shoulder, leaving it with a little pat.

"Too many stars make me dizzy."

I went quickly to the door, switched on the light, went round the lobby and all three rooms switching on lights, even the light on the balcony. We must have blazed out over the valley.

"You can stop looking now, dammit! Final curtain."

She turned round then, not looking at me but at the door.

"I guess so."

"I'll tell Rick when he comes back that you went early. Headache. Altitude."

"Went?"

"When he comes back from the—"

She blushed vividly from breast to hair and it was only then, I swear, that I saw the pattern of their collusion. Her voice thinned to a little girl's voice.

"No—I—thank you for having me."

She ran towards the door, running clumsily as if she weren't seeing straight. Suddenly I felt as I might have felt, yes, might have felt but never did, for Emily.

"Mary Lou—"

She delayed, half-turned, and red in the face. As if she were put back to her teens—the day before yesterday—she rasied her right hand to shoulder height and wiggled the fingers at me.

"'Bye for now."

After that, without any help, she got herself through the door of the sitting-room and through the lobby and the outside door and—the carpet on the floor of the short corridor was too thick to let me hear if she ran or walked or staggered along it.

What did he expect? What was the, as we say in our jargon, projected scenario? Did he think we would fence archly, and she, girlishly, dodge round the table and say, no, Wilf, no, not unless you sign that paper? Or was she to crawl up me odalisquelike to plead with her lips pouted? Or was she to agree in a matter-of-fact way like a noseblow and then I, obligated, would sign, saying, take it, it's what you want.

Thank you for having me! The pathetic idiocy, the vulnerability of the girl, the gross, insulting imperceptivity of the man! Yet he had not been so very far out after all. Had that skin been warm and given back the faintest signal, how different it would all have been! Neither of us, critic and author, we knew nothing about people or not enough. We knew about paper, that was all. The poor girl was the human one. She didn't know how to do it. But then—I didn't know how to do it! He didn't know how to offer it. Pimp, client and whore, all we three needed the assistance of a professional. I stood in the blazing room, behind me the dark oblong of the window with its quenched stars. I stared at Rick's paper on the table, then at the card hung on the outer door, *Avis aux MM les clients.* I thought of Rick lying discreetly in bed, perhaps snoring gently so as to make his wife's return something neither of them need take notice of or comment on. But she would shake him out of his snores and assure him that nothing had happened, nothing at all except that Mr Barclay had put his hand on her left shoulder, yes, shoulder, and she knew he wanted her only he hadn't done anything but taken his hand away again and he hadn't said much, nothing had happened, nothing at all, would he hold her, please, please, make love to her, she was so, so soiled and he must never, never ask her again—

Then at last they would sleep, her tears hung in the thickets of his chest.

The paper was still on the table. *I hereby appoint Professor Rick L. Tucker. . . .*

I could make him suffer. I could sign it and give it to him tomorrow when we went walking.

"Mary Lou forgot this, Rick. By Jove, she earned it!"

Unspeakable! The vision of her, the glamour and the childish vulnerability caught me by the heart and the throat, nowhere else, it seemed. But there was a touch of panic too. I knew that the finger was on me, I was limed by her and would have to struggle to get myself free. Only the space of one day, morning, noon, night, to bring such change! It was there, the trap I had tried to avoid—and *would* avoid!—the bitter sorrow of a love that is fruitless, pointless, hopeless, agonizing and ridiculous. Once more, the clown's trousers had fallen down.

I cursed myself inwardly, then protested to myself that all was not lost. The brandy was still on the table, the mature man's consolation. Then, paper man that I am, I began to think—what a story!

Chapter VIII

I woke too early with a clear memory of the night before and the kind of parched distancing from reality which comes from considerable brandy. After the bathroom I went into the sitting-room and was not surprised to see that the brandy bottle was half empty. Strangely, though, apart from dryness, I had no hangover. Instead I had a thirst which I quenched with about six successive tumblers of mountain water. It seemed rather immoral to have drunk so much and not to be suffering for it, but the fact was undeniable, I was feeling physically as well as I had ever felt in my life. Rage and sorrow burn up alcohol. I remembered and examined my new thraldom and rebelled against it. *Think no more of her is always the solution.* For she had committed herself, there was no doubt of it, consented to shape her life on completing with him a charmed circle. It was all the more evident from the ludicrous and sordid non-transaction of the night before. Think no more of her, put that image out of the visualizing eye, for God's sake, don't be your age, that way madness lies. Think rather of him and his attempt at *liming* a literary bird—

Well. I would teach Professor Tucker a lesson he would never forget. I would take to my own weapons. I would put him in a book, a story, with such a viciously precise delineation that even Mary Lou would blush for him and the strange rich man Halliday laugh him out of his life.

Then, of course, the novelist's truism popped out. It was no good putting the real, live Rick L. Tucker in a book. He had this in common with most of the human race—he was quite spectacularly unbelievable. There are things that novelists invent which they call characters but they aren't.

They're constructs, shaved down out of some wood or other—a psychic plasma—into figures as like each other as Russian dolls. The only thing I could do was select, tone down, adjust, produce a comically loathsome figure, recognizable and tolerable because it was "only a story".

It came to me—and with an eighth glass of water—that I must do what I had never done before in my life. No more invention, only selection—I must actually study a living person. Jake should become my prey. Instead of trying to avoid him when boredom or anger set in, I must reverse our situation. All the time he thought he was finding out about me I should be finding out about him. It was all the exhilaration of the hunt. Yoicks! Tally ho!

All the time, over breakfast then dressing, I was busy putting together what I knew of him and realized at last that it amounted to less than the police would want for a description. He was large, he was huge—how huge? The tall young man who had crouched behind our dustbin had filled out in every way. He was broad and thick. I called to mind the mat of hair, the forest of hair, I had seen all down his front. As well as that, there were thickets in his arm pits, small images of the same in his nostrils—probably the hair extended down his legs to end round his ankles like the feathers on a cob or, rather more aptly, on a cart horse. It grew thick and close over his head, thick on his eyebrows, thick and long as eyelashes. Had the hairy Ainu crossed by way of the frozen Bering Straits, or had later immigration brought this near-freak the other way across the Atlantic? Examined, rather than run from or derided, I began to see that Professor Tucker was not without interest. How much hair could the novelist get away with? Not quite so much—the bit down the front, the mop of black hair on his head, the eyebrows and eyelashes would be more than enough. Mostly the writer deals with the bits of his characters that stick out. The rest is silence—clothes, I mean. It was sheer luck I knew he was as shaggy between the legs as a Shetland pony.

Skin. Oddly white, in itself, but where a beard and

moustache might have been the area was covered with the black roots of hairs all cut off by pressure of the safety razor just, as it were, below ground level but still there and visible, giving, with the white, slightly oily skin, an effect of—what? Absurdly, my mind could find nothing but a quotation from somewhere, a quotation the aptness of which was not apparent—*silence and old night*.

Hands, square, fat, white, the backs inevitably sprinkled with the standard Tuckerish hair. And so clean. Far too clean, the nails very nearly convex rather than—hell, which was which? They were dished, would hold rain water.

He must be strong, of course. One of those hands could squeeze—made into a fist could hit—or wielding an axe—but they had never done so. The typewriter was their weapon.

Those shaggy privates—no. Learn, old man, what is not to be thought, not to be touched on, what is nothing, nothing but sickness and pain. Forget. Let it be.

So. To the hunt!

Mary Lou?

I would avoid her as much as possible, only tolerating them until I had all the relevant information on my pursuer. I would suffer a little but then she would be gone.

Rick and I met in the foyer. I was in moderately heavy boots and anorak, Rick dressed, except for the skates, as if he were about to play ice hockey. He looked enormous. OLE ASHCAN was to the fore again. Yes, he *was* enormous.

"How tall are you, Rick?"

"A metre—"

"Old style, please."

"Six feet three inches, sir."

"And you weigh—not in kilos but pounds?"

"Two hundred twenty-five."

"Could you divide that by fourteen?"

He did so. I whistled.

"And you look it, Rick, every hunkish pound. What on earth got you stuck with academics?"

80

"I wanted it, Wilf. Wilf, those boots, they wouldn't last over rough country."

"They are not going to be taken over rough country."

"Maybe not today, but—"

"Have you noticed?"

"Yeah. Fog."

"They don't advertise it."

"No, sir, they don't. Wilf, I was really sorry not to see the stars with you last night. Mary Lou said it was truly inspirational."

"She did? Well, today we can see all of twenty-five yards. We are down to earth, Rick."

"Am I going too fast for you, Wilf?"

"Not yet but it's a kind thought."

"Maybe you wondered why I didn't join you last night?"

Mindful of my new role as hunter, I nodded.

"Yes, why?"

"We take this path to the left. My God, the fog's thickening, Wilf. But don't worry, there's a handrail all the way. Even if the fog closes right in, we can feel along the cliff edge—"

"Christ!"

"I didn't say anything last night, Wilf, but the altitude got to me too."

"You're like her, Rick, you're just not physical. I've never met such a truly spiritual pair. But this cliff: I warn you, I don't like heights. I don't even like that bloody balcony."

"Come to that, Wilf, I don't like the way these fields smell."

"Stink. Doctor Johnson."

"Fertilizer."

"It's shit, you fool. It doesn't disappear for ever in the John and Jean. It's human. They spread it around. They don't waste anything."

Rick gagged and clapped a handful of Kleenex over his mouth and nose. He broke into a canter and soon disappeared into the fog a few yards further along the path. I peered up into the fog and could detect slightly more luminosity in it in one direction than another. Presumably the sun was up there still and moving towards midday. Later perhaps I should be able to see the cliff and decide whether I would go on or not. Meanwhile I strolled slowly between malodorous and invisible fields. I took my time. Some people can't stand heights. Others can't stand faeces. *Chacun* et cetera.

Ten minutes later there was the hygienic smell of pines and the suggestion round me of their massive darknesses in the fog. Rick was waiting for me. At that point the air was clearing a trifle, so that as soon as I saw him I also saw tree tops on my left at eye level and pine roots in a bank on my right. Rick, I now saw, was leaning negligently against a railing on the left-hand side of the path.

"Aw, Wilf—it's solid as the rock."

Nevertheless he heaved himself upright, adjusted his pace to mine. There was the sound of water rushing down the mountain somewhere ahead. It was strangely comforting, heaven knows why. I stared up into the fog and could make out now and then a silver penny racing through intense whiteness and inanity towards the zenith. I looked down and round me. The three tops had withdrawn, suggesting some increasing gap of air below us on the left.

"Are you sure this path is OK, Rick? You've been along it? A solid rail all the way? No nasty surprises?'

"No, sir."

We walked on together. The rushing sound was nearer and presently water came into view. It was a small mountain stream that dropped out of the fog on the right, splashed across the path and disappeared into the fog below us. Rick stopped before the stream. He raised a finger, hushing me. I stopped and hushed. He had more black hairs in his right nostril than the left. He was right-nostrilled.

There was nothing to hear but the stream and, faintly

somewhere, cowbells. I sat by the stream on a convenient projection of rock. I looked up at him, raising my eyebrows. For answer he pointed to the stream. I listened again, bent down and pretended to smell it, put a finger in but took it out again quickly, fearing frost bite.

"Can't you hear, Wilf?"

"Course I can."

"I mean—isn't there something real queer about the sound?"

"No."

"Listen again."

It was true. The stream, a single skein of falling water briefly interrupted by the path, had two voices, not one. There was the cheerful babble, a kind of frivolity as if the thing, the Form, enjoyed its bounding passage downward, through space. Then running under that was a deep, meditative hum as if despite the frivolity and surface prattle the thing sounded from some deep secret of the mountain itself.

"It's not just single!"

"Yeah. 'Two voices are there, one is of the deep—'"

I looked at him with surprise that turned to an unwilling degree of respect. There had been last night—and now this.

"I've never listened to water before—not really listened."

"I can't believe that, Wilf."

Also, my mind noted and put away in some drawer to be taken out later that there was a lengthy piece of prose to be written on listening to natural sound—listening without comment or presupposition.

"How come, Rick, as you might say? I mean why you?"

"I'm not making the connection, Wilf."

"Listening to a stream!"

"I know how I must seem to you, sir. Just another sincere but limited academic."

"Oh my! Oh my giddy aunt! Golly! Dash it!"

"I mean it, Wilf."

"Straightforward. Sincere. A man incapable of—"

But Rick had gone on as if something I had not known in him had been touched.

"I do listen. I always have done. Birds, wind, water—the different sounds of water. Sometimes I think in the sea you can hear the salt. The difference, I mean."

"The great outdoors."

"Surely. Then sometimes, you know, you lie awake and listen to no noise, though that's rare nowadays—but sometimes you can listen to no noise—positive no noise and go out and out and out, searching—"

"Nature mysticism."

"No, sir. It's just how living is. Then there's music. Oh my God. But I hadn't the talent."

"Had to settle for the groves of academe."

"Yeah. No—I mean, sincerely no!"

"Let's get on."

Rick came towards me, his cleft chin out where it belonged now, as if the sound of water was a cure for diffidence. I had one of those moments, not so much of thought as rapid reflection, a split second in which possibilities, alternatives were considered and dismissed. I dismissed. Was a cleft chin a sign of weakness? No. Was it the sign of a divided nature? Absurd. Was it a delay in the hardening of the bones, a hint of foetalism, as the biological boys used to say and perhaps still did?

He held out his hand, and it seemed natural to take hold and allow myself to be pulled up off the low rock. The careful Swiss had inlaid hollow trunks in the road so that though the path sloped slightly up, the water ran straight across it. To get across was no more than a step. We crossed into a place where it seemed there was no solidity but a dimly seen rail on the left hand and tree roots on the other.

I stood still.

"For a scenic stroll, it's spectacularly null."

"This'll clear."

"If it weren't for the silence, we might be strolling in

84

Regent's Park. I come here in expectation of scenery and all I get is a white-out."

"The manager said it was unusual for the time of the year."

"Every two hundred years."

"You're putting me on."

"I must have been to dozens of places where they swore to me it was the worst weather for two hundred years. Always two hundred years. Cairo, Tbilisi—"

"Now, now!"

"Remind me to tell you some time about the highest tide for two hundred years."

"Tell me about the highest tide for two hundred years."

"I crewed for a man once in his yacht. Highest tide for two hundred years. I ran him aground on it."

Rick laughed, a genuine, unservile, happy laugh.

"If he was skipper, it was his doing."

"No, no. I claim the distinction. Curse this fog."

"We start climbing again soon. I guess we'll climb out of it."

"Quote, mother, give me the sun, unquote."

"The medics say he got his facts wrong."

"He got everything wrong. Stagey old twit."

Rick gave a scandalized guffaw. He was having a real good time. I could see his mental notebook. All the same—

"I know! I know! Gee!"

"Like Wagner."

The guffaw prolonged itself. There was a sudden extraordinary twisting of the vapour before our faces, a humming sound in the air, a wooden knock on the left, then somewhere down in the fog a mighty thump.

"Oh my!"

"It's the mountain, Rick," I said, not yet too scared to play the imperturbable or, if you like, insensitive Englishman. "It's the bloody mountain, old fellow. He, she or it is throwing rocks at us. We ought to be flattered. Are you flattered?"

"I want out."

85

He turned to go but I caught his sleeve.

"This is a sheer gift for a writer. Just think, Rick. Now we can describe what it sounds like to be missed by a cannon ball. What wouldn't Tennyson have given?"

"We better get back, Wilf."

"What's the hurry?"

"There's no knowing what might be going on up above, Wilf. I know mountains. I was born—why, it could be a real slip, real dangerous."

"Currently."

"Yeah."

"As of this moment in time."

"Yeah."

"The lightning never strikes twice in the same place. We ought to see where it struck."

Securely prevented by the dense fog from experiencing the hideousness of the drop, still unperturbed and wishing to *show* this young man who had unexpectedly revealed a too profound concern for his own safety, I stepped to the rail.

"Aw—c'mon Wilf!"

"I can't see a thing."

Still unperturbed, I put my hand on the rail and leaned out. The rail went with me.

The next few seconds can be described in a few words or a few hundred. My instinct—voluble as ever—is for the hundreds. It's not just that I make my money by selling words but that these seconds were very important seconds as far as I was concerned. The first of them, I have to confess, was an hiatus, a nothing. The second was a contraction, a shock too immediate to be called belief or even apprehension. It was, if you like, the animal body's awareness, alerted to death so near, the falling to it. The third second was more human in a way—the rail now moving out and down faster and more easily—was blind terror which I became, awareness of blind terror, blind terror aware of itself and, shot through the terror, incredulity. Then the animal took over, every nerve, muscle, heart beat, at top energy and speed, bent on denial of destruction. My wits were gone. My hand, as it clutched and fell with the rail, was vitalized to the point where it might well have squeezed the wood small to its own crippling deformation but nowhere was the wit that would have made me let the thing go. My other hand struck out blindly to where there might be solidity, found it, clutched what felt like a plant and my body turned head over heels so that I landed against the cliff on the other side of the rail with a blow that knocked the breath out of me. The rail dropped away from my one hand as the shock opened it for me. That hand, without asking any permission, grabbed. I was on my back, heels dug in, hands gripped. I was sliding steeply, inch by inch.

A hand was holding me by the collar at the back of my neck. I stopped sliding and inspected the red blotches and blurs that whirled before my eyes and were all I could see. There were, I now felt in every nerve and artery, five points of attachment and support between me and smash. Four of these points were only minimally effective, hands and heels dug into soft earth, left hand clutching a sappy stem, right hand scrabbled into wet mud. Then there was the choking grip of a fist on the suede collar at the back of my neck. The four other points of attachment might be a help, but there was no doubt that I was suspended chiefly from the fist so hard against my nape. That was what held me in this opaque and pendant space. As for the world, but just now so silent, it was noisy with the thumping of my heart, the roaring in my ears and the gasps that came as of themselves out of my chest. Terror was as much an element as space. Here was no dalliance of the mind with the worthlessness or worth of life. The animal knew beyond all question what was precious beyond everything. All that was conscious was a wish that wished itself, for the terror—like the bombing, the shooting, the soughing of shells—to stop. Behind and beyond the fist someone else was gasping too.

I was moving down. The gasps behind me quickened. I

dared to shift a heel and dig it in an inch or two higher, but
the soil slid away and I felt how the effort had diminished
the friction that helped to keep me from falling into the
fog.

Rick articulated.

"Hold still."

I stopped moving down.

"Root above left hand."

I dared to let go of the plant slowly and allowed my
fingers to crawl. The root was there, thick, slimy but
graspable because of its contortions.

"Pull."

There was undreamed of strength in my left hand. The
only limit was the strength of the root. I could have lifted
myself with anvils hanging from my feet.

"Turn over—real slow."

I did that, and the fist turned with me, my collar twisting
but not too much. Now there was something to see. There
was perhaps eighteen inches of earth, coarse grass, small
stones and small roots. The slope was close to the vertical.
Rick was flat on the path, his left hand hooked round the
upright post that had held one end of the fallen bar. His
right hand held my collar. The upright post was bowing
outwards very slowly, earth and stone dropping from its
base.

"Jesus!"

Rick articulated again.

"I won't let go."

Inch by inch. I had such hope of safety now that the
mixture of hope and fear was almost more agonizing than
the instant terror, for Rick was moving with the post, it
was what held him, that and his weight against my
weight. We were looking each other in the face, an eyeball
confrontation, his beneath a frowning forehead. He
seemed extraordinarily calm, as if this idiot caper played
with our destruction was a small problem of tax or admin.

Inch by inch. Heel, fingers, hand, fist— Then I had a
hand on the path, then an elbow, then I lurched forward

88

on one knee as the post fell and thumped somewhere in the fog. We were tangled on the path. I scrambled across it and my body huddled itself against the roots and solid rock of the mountainside. I didn't say anything. I began first to crawl, then stagger, back along that path, keeping close to the left-hand side like a tramp or a drunk needing the security of a wall beside him. I stumbled through the little stream and fell on the rock where I had sat. I could see Rick's boots in front of me. The deeper voice of the stream had consumed the lighter one. It was as if the mountain was speaking with the same deep tone that had been audible and now, in the mind, *visible* round the falling lump of rock. I started to giggle.

"Shiver and shake. Alfred Lord Tennyson."

"Take it easy, Wilf. You'll be all right."

Of course he would know, Eng. Lit. and all that. Shiver and shake along the country road, a treat for the local lads.

It seemed to me that I could feel the indifferent threat of the earth through the soles of my feet, the volcanoes, earthquakes, tsunamis, terrors of nature's fact, the ball flying through space. That was what the water spoke of, not *Gaia Mater* but the space rock balanced between forces so that gravity exhibited itself with this ghastly indifference.

"Here."

Irresistible hands were grasping me. I rose, as it might be propelled by a force of nature, I came against wool and warmth. There was strain in my arms. My cheek was ground into skin, hair, the muscles of a neck. We were moving slowly at first, then briskly. A horse, a horse! That huge creature had my passive body in charge, had lifted me into its aura of strength and warmth. It was the warmth that was most disconcerting, now another human manifestation like the smell of shit that stung my nostrils, for he was cantering, there is no other word for it, down through the meadows and into the home stretch. Then I was being lowered. There were voices and other hands and presently I was in my own bed. I opened my eyes saw two thick columns of trouser, and at the juncture of those columns the bulging flies above me. I shut my eyes again. I heard him move and dared a look through one eye. Now he stood at the foot of the bed, looking down. There was a slight smile round his lips. I thought it was friendly enough but there was something else in it. The smile widened.

I shut my one eye again. There was no doubt at all. The smile was a smile of triumph.

"You OK?"

The manager was at his shoulder. They consulted. Rick talked of brandy.

I interrupted him in a voice which I heard was normal enough.

"I don't want brandy. I want hot chocolate."

Nursery stuff. But the manager hurried away. Now I was sitting up, my shoulders felt as if they had been racked. Every now and then I had the shakes again. A sensitive type, Wilf Barclay! I shut my eyes, screwed them up and endured the agony of this added link in some chain of farce, this unbudgeted addition to a whole store of recurrent memories, the time Wilf Barclay fell off a cliff and was held up by—

"I didn't lose my trousers. I hadn't a round, red nose and ginger hair and a painted squint."

"Lie down again, Wilf."

"The very thing, the last bleeding—the only bloody thing that could have happened to reverse everything. How do I do it? What does it? Oh fuck!"

"You better lie down."

The manager hurried back. He had a cup and saucer. Rick took it from him. The manager hurried away. From outside I heard Mary Lou's voice.

"Should I come in?"

I shouted, "No!"

Rick put the cup down on the little bedside table. I came over dizzy and lay back. There was a long pause in which doors opened and shut several times, then another pause.

90

A heavily accented German voice spoke by me.

"He is in some shock, I think. The chocolate was good. The body has its own voice."

Then I realized that my pulse was being taken. The voice spoke again.

"It is not so bad. How old? *That* old! Well. Drink your chocolate, Mr Barclay. Professor Tucker? Yes. Just rest, I think. He has the physique of a far younger man."

I could hear Rick muttering. The doctor spoke again.

"I will send something. Yes, now, it is only a few yards. Do please remember, even in the Weisswald we say the green fields kill more than the white."

But under my shut eyelids I was stretching antennae of horror out to the edge of the universe. The dice were rolling, three sixes or three ones. They were large as planets.

"I'll wait to give you the stuff, Wilf."

He was large as a planet, entering my universe with his necessity and his warmth and his smile and dainty bed-piece all drawn along by that gravity of an ambition not worth suffering for. I opened my eyes to get away from the rolling dice and there he was, large as his life, smiling anxiously by the foot of the bed. I examined myself and found I was in vest and shirt. I sat up, lifted the cup and saucer to me as they rattled against each other. I did not care to look at him.

"Let me—"

"Leave me alone!"

Ungrateful bugger, Wilf Barclay, and now enjoying his ingratitude the way he might enjoy cruelty if he had the courage. Ingratitude and sadism all mixed up—what nonsense! But Professor Tucker still stood there, while my cup and saucer rattled in my hands and I managed at last to drink. It did immediately calm me with its nursery taste and nursery memories. I was able, as they say, to take a hold of myself. I went on drinking until I had finished the lot, then held it out to Rick.

"More."

He did look a bit startled then and the smile went stiff. All the same he took the cup and saucer and went away. I sat with my painful arms round my knees. It had started down in Schwillen when—of all things!—I had felt lonely and had not been enjoying it—*I*, Wilf Barclay, a specialist in loneliness if ever there was one! I chewed over the steps that had put me in this position of all that I had not wanted to find myself in. The door of the bedroom was open and I could see beyond it, in the sitting-room, how Rick's *billet-doux* lay on the table still, unsigned, unmoved. My shakes and memories began to be consumed by another feeling that at least restored some personality to me. It was a tide of sheer fury. When Rick came back with another steaming cup I flung over on the pillow and would not look at him. I muttered my accusation.

"It seems I owe you my life."

Chapter IX

Fury, hatred and fear. Somewhere in my paroxysm I was so fierce with him that he took himself off and I was there in my shirt and pants, shaking like a machine with a part missing. First his wife, then when that ploy failed, my life, my own damned, sweet, secret possession, handed back to me, but now, as I saw, on conditions like the surrender of a city. Also there was something else to add—a physical detestation of his strength and warmth and stink!

It was the manager who brought me dope from the doctor and I sank into a sleep beyond dreams, still making plans, such as tempting them both to a cliff. There's no doubt about it. Shock had unbalanced my mechanism. At one point I had Tucker writing my biography but with such strict supervision it included for the world's inspection an account of how he had attempted the virtue of St Wilfred with the offer of his beautiful wife; an offer rejected with such gentle tact and kindness that he (Assistant Professor Rick L. Tucker) flung himself on his knees and received such a gigantic hack in his privates from one of those boots that were no good for rough country he immediately entered a monastery, leaving his beautiful wife to—

Yes, I was unbalanced, there's no doubt about it. But the dope was good and I wish I knew what it was.

I woke with aching shoulders and a blank mind. I looked at my watch and it took me some time to work out that today was in fact tomorrow. My mouth tasted as if it were lined with nasty metal. I washed it with cold water for a long time. My legs were inclined to give way. With the memory of the day before there came very little fury or hatred. All that came of those weird sisters was fear, not to say panic. As if recovery from the dope implied that I was on my own and open now for business, I saw the dreadful results of giving Rick any permission whatever—that determined, sedulous search into a past raw with unforgiving memories! That girl impossible for me, such a danger, such a grief!

The paper was still there, lying on a newly dusted and polished table. Had the fat, grey-haired woman dusted round it, or had she lifted it carefully, dusted, polished, then replaced it with the precision of a referee putting back a snooker ball? There the paper was.

It seems I owe you my life.

That brought me to, like the school bell. I owed him my life, nothing less. It was like every boy's story that ever was.

"I owe you my life, old man."

"That's all right, old fellow. It was nothing."

"Your arm's broken, old man."

"It's not my right arm, old fellow."

It was sheer, low comedy all over again.

Well, there the paper was. I turned my attention away from it and into myself. Wilfred Barclay didn't fit into any boy's adventure story, only into a parody of one: and even then not as the hero or the hero's little chum with whom junior could empathize, but perhaps as a small-time crook put in to demonstrate that crime does not pay or that virtue does. He would get laid out with a straight left. Wilfred Barclay would reel away, holding his jaw and vowing filthy revenge. He would never be fool enough to sign that paper. He would have taken the wife and scarpered.

Scarper!

Never mind the wife. There are wives everywhere. Anyway, had I deceived myself? Had she ever been offered to St Wilfred? Careful! Was I mad? Was Rick mad? There was an intensity at times about his stare, white showing all round the pupils, as if he were about to charge dangerously. A psychiatrist would find him interesting.

To hell with a careful examination of him. His hair—he was *disgusting*. It would be less risky to keep tabs on a rhinoceros. This was a mad house and Wilfred Barclay, St Wilfred, no longer a character in a boy's book, would do a bit of levitation, gravitation. He would not bow out, he would simply disappear, vanish down the rack railway, hey presto!

As soon as I had decided that, my heart became high and giggly. I had not known till then what a strain sheer companionship had been. I got hold of the manager and found that the Tuckers had gone walking. I explained myself. After the shock I needed solitude. Though I had booked in for a week, I must go now. (I promised him compensation—a full meed of praise for him and the hotel in a book! I do, in fact, some years after, I forget how many, discharge that debt. The hotel Felsenblick, Weisswald, Switzerland, is comfortable, the view superb, the drop ghastly. You will find Major Adolf Kaufmann, a very retired general by now, unobtrusive and silent.) The fat woman packed for me and carried my bags to the rack railway, where I caught the three o'clock descent. So I escaped, leaving behind me as forwarding address The Hotel, Akureyri, Iceland. Three hours after I was in a plane bound for Florence and another hire car. By early evening I was driving through the Apennines on my national home, an autostrada. I was calm, watching the motionless landscape stream past. I was surrounded by metal and I was my own master. That night I spent in a sleazy hotel a biscuit toss from La Rotonda. I remember the joy and freedom with which I flung up my window, gazed out on the magnificent shadow and invented quite unfair bits of dialogue for Mr and Mrs Rick.

"There's a great hole in the roof, hon."

"That's bomb damage, I guess, hon."

I was myself again. I slept soundly.

Next morning I was not really worried again but a bit preoccupied. After all, La Rotonda is a place like Piccadilly or Time Square where, they say, you'll meet anybody if you wait long enough. It's an oblique way of saying that a lot of people go there. Once Rick and Mary Lou had lost the scent—even Rick had more wit than to go to Iceland—Rome was likely. Go thou to Rome! He would do it. Had he not said Mary Lou simply had to see Rome and Dublin? A flash of the glamour made me catch my breath. There was no guarantee that she had not yet *done* Rome or that, having done it, she would not want to do it again. I was in Navona and sitting at another round metal table or the same metal table when my heart, as they say, turned over. No. I didn't see Mary Lou, I saw Rick. I saw Rick in the same way I used *very nearly to see* Elizabeth in the old days when I still cared enough. That is to say, I did not *see* Rick precisely. But I came to with a jump that would have spilt the coffee if I had not just drunk it.

"Christ!"

It was entirely possible. They could have left straight after their walk, then flown direct from Zurich to Rome in the evening or overnight or that very morning. I would have been safer on my motor road. I wasn't seeing. I was remembering with an etched precision. Only this wasn't a memory swimming up, as it were, from the depths. It was a kind of time slip or time shift, or like the "click" with which you can substitute one slide for another, then click back to the first one. It was a moment at which I had to pause and refuse to credit Rick with more than method and determination. He was not a ghost, worse luck. He was not a saint with powers of transportation and bilocation. He had been there in the Piazza Navona! He had just inspected the fountain, probably identifying the mythologized rivers. He had been turning away, still putting his tiny camera to rights under the cuff of his sweater on the right arm. I had not seen the front of that sweater with OLE ASHCAN knitted into the chest but I had seen the very beginnings of the O. What was more, less than forty-eight hours before, my nose had been resting in the disgusting heat of the sweater at the back of his neck when he carried me down through the alp from that damned mountain path. I knew it well enough and his huge shoes and his hair, discreetly long as befits a serious academic. He had gone away, vanished down a street on the other side from the café. If I had not been in a dream at the completeness of my escape from involvement, I would have started up and run before he vanished. Or I could have tracked him to his hotel, where the golden cloud of glamour was still lying in, not being physical.

I jumped up, shoved some money on the little table and hurried away, keeping a weather eye round most points of the compass, which enabled me to see the sinister speed with which a passing dropout removed my money from the table before the waiter could reach it. I kept assuring myself that I had not been mistaken—could not be mistaken. Oh yes, I remembered the line of Rick's shoulder, his arm, his trousers made from the latest spinoff and those thick-soled imperial hoofers with which tourists keep a distance between themselves and the land they tread on. Yes. If I hadn't been so preoccupied with calm pleasure in a sense of anonymity, I might even have seen him face to face. At this point I realized that my sense of security could not have influenced Rick. He would have seen me whether I had seen him or not. Or had I developed the chameleon's power? Had I looked like an iron chair or a stretch of stone wall?

The sunglasses! That was why the morning sun was now trying my eyes! I had picked them up next door to the hotel when I strolled over. They had hidden all of my face except for my scraggy beard, and beards in Rome were thick as buttercups in a field. I must have been unrecognizable as a professional gentleman gathering evidence for divorce or espionage or shoplifting; and now, damn it, doubtless startled by remembering Rick, I remembered leaving them on the usual iron table. *The* round metal table. I thought for a moment that it would be too dangerous to return to Navona and get my spectacles back; but then I sneaked up on the square carefully, as a professional gent, and peered round the corner. Yes, my sunglasses were gone. There had been a raid by another dropout.

I felt very confused and by midday I had left the hotel (forwarding address: The Confederate Hotel, Roanoke, VA) and was driving in a direction which I thought would fox any pursuer. I drove east, reckoning that sideroads were the thing, so soon after the *annulare* I got on to them.

But if it wasn't coincidence, how on earth could Rick have found out? If he were going on the evidence, he would now be on his way to Iceland. Certainly I had told no one. Customs had been indifferent, a young man who opened the passport and shut it again without looking—or had that been deliberate, to lull me into a *sense* of his indifference?

It was then that I slowed up and pulled into an open space at an elbow of road. I parked and switched off the engine. I said, Wilfred Barclay, you are still in shock. You should have waited a couple of days. Mary Lou had to see Rome and Dublin. They would see Rome, regretting perhaps that poor old Wilf had disappeared so inexplicably, but then it's not just being a Brit, it's being a writer. Put the two together, Mary Lou, and you just don't know *what* they'll do, rushing off. Why, look at Shelley and Noël Coward. No, hon, not together, separately. Hon, I know you majored in Eng. Lit., you were my favourite pupil, natch, oh I get it, it's like poor Wilf would say, you're tugging my leg. No, he'd say, you're approaching my lower limbs with a view to exerting some traction. Ha Ha. Ha Ha Ha Ha. Ha Ha. Ha Ha. Ha Ha. Ha Ha. But what's Mr Halliday going to say? From that point of view it's real unkind of Wilf. After all, we only wanted to know about his past, particularly the juicy bits, and the occasional crime, let alone the infinite number of times he's made a private clown of himself, what makes him tick in fact. He's no right to hide any of that, hon. Why shouldn't we make a meal of him?

What would *she* say? Somehow I didn't seem able to invent speeches for the glamour. But Rick was easy.

98

Hon, I ought to say I never meant you any harm. The altitude really did get to me. Affected my judgement, I guess. But I knew you'd be safe, he'd turn you down. He's one of *them*, hon. Got a hang-up. My guess, you could call it an insight, hon, is that he's never had anything to do with women at all. An invert. After all, hon, his mother brought him up and he was educated at a British private school and you know what that means. Now, hon, it's time you got out of bed, we got to do St Peter's before one, hon.

I was amused by my poor invention and felt better. I told myself I was making heavy weather of the whole thing. After Rome they would go to Dublin and walk the stations of poor old Bloom.

The billionaire, Halliday. Mary Lou admired him evidently, in her innocence. Wealth is a secondary sexual characteristic, like talent, like genius. I wondered for a while if I should drive back to Rome and look up Mr Halliday in the appropriate reference book but decided against it.

So at last I was able to trundle on, almost fancy-free and secure. There is one thing, though, that I noticed about myself. It was an indulgence. I feared to be the object of a biography. At the same time I was—no matter how hard I tried not to be—I was flattered by the possibility. Every time my mind flinched from some raw wound of my past it took refuge in a contemplation of my present distinction. Then, paring that same distinction down and down, reminding myself of this and that—of this writer and that writer—in the end my mind would be left with a faint feeling of the valuable, the unusual and the august. I caught myself gazing through new dark glasses and under my panama at groups of English tourists and telling myself, *if they only knew!* So I trundled on, or sat at my round white table and drank. It came to me—this was in a hotel near Aquila which was an escape place in the hot weather for Italians—it came to me that such a man could *show* Halliday and Rick Tucker—such a man was, in fact bigger than he had thought—thank you, Professor Tucker! Hold this one! I remember sitting and, as they used to say, discussing a very tolerable bottle of wine and watching the sun set in the general direction of Rome, and deciding that I was at peace because I knew precisely the book I was going to write. It would extend the Barclay range. It would deal with simple, eternal things, youth and innocence, purity and love. I bought a typewriter at once. The place was quiet. No one spoke to me except in the ways of most minimal courtesy. Liking sex but being incapable of love, indeed! Calmly, perhaps even augustly, I composed my book.

So there Helen Davenant and young Ivo Clark rode their horses through the green fields of an English countryside that I was hard put to remember with anything like accuracy. Not that it matters, of course. *Horses at the Spring* is as much a pastoral as *Daphnis and Chloë* or one of Virgil's Eclogues. I remember I was deeply moved by it myself. Helen owed something to Mary Lou—a kind of clumsy goodness, painstaking and ignorant, her innocence complete. Ivo, I don't mind admitting, was that groom who had once been a bank clerk and I had to do a fair cleaning-up job on him. It was all so easy to write and so enjoyable! I have found out that the critical reaction was adverse (they said it stank) but I don't think it was really as bad as all that. I had a very peaceful time. With modest triumph, though, and some regret, I let the manuscript go to my agent. I gave him a poste restante in Yugoslavia, then hung about, waiting for a reply, in Titograd which is where no tourists go.

The result was I got a whole load of stuff out from England. The first thing that arrived before the rest was a telegram from Liz. ONCE AGAIN WHAT AM I TO DO WITH YOUR BLOODY PAPERS QUESTION MARK THEY ARE INCREASING DAILY HUMPH OBJECTS HOPE THIS FINDS YOU AS IT LEAVES ME EMMY SENDS WISHES. LIZ. The next was an enthusiastic telegram from my agent full of congratulations and saying he was having the MS retyped.

I was very chuffed by the news and thought even better of myself. Liking sex but incapable of love, indeed!

Ha et cetera.

Then a hundredweight or so of mail turned up. I was getting tired of drinking Dingaç, which is the most fattening wine in the world and filthy sweet. So I took the lot back to Italy and sorted through. The only interesting thing was a deliberately reasonable letter (not telegram—the letter had been written before) from Liz. Would I keep the Tuckers off her back? Rick must be working for Pinkerton's! She didn't mind Humphrey making passes at Mary Lou, she was resigned to male nature and the leopard (a touch of unconscious humour there, I fancy) would never be shot of his spots. But she was afraid that Rick had been seeing Emmy in London. Did I remember Emmy? (Heavy sarcasm.) Emmy had suffered enough, was to be blunt not the sort of young woman normally attractive to men, and she felt that Rick was using her as a stalking horse, or one of the "hides" Humph kept on about, for keeping an eye on me: or even to screw (an unconscious pun probably) out of her memories of me as dad. Rick had a project and she must tell me the crown of his life's work would be a biography of me, poor Wilf, but before that he was working on Wilfred Barclay, a Source Book. It was a pity the man Halliday couldn't find a better use for his money but power corrupts and all that. She hoped wherever I was I had found happiness and (a real Liz touch) I had certainly spent enough time, money and people running after it. Now the bitterness was over she'd come to see that I'd been generous in allowing her to keep her share of the limited company, she didn't know what she and Humph let alone Emmy would have done without it, he didn't do a hand's turn, a man's man. P. P. S. Kestrel had had to be put down sorry, she hoped I was happy with whoever I was with. She wasn't well.

I read and reread that letter because it contained so much, most of which had to be inferred. Not well! Who could be, living with that bastard? There's no doubt,

women ought to have their marriages arranged for them—
my God, the bastards they hook on to blithely! They—I
used to think it served her right, him I mean, but after
years of not caring, now I felt genuinely sorry for her;
however, enough is enough. What was more important
was Rick. God almighty! Pinkerton's! It scared me so
much, no matter how much I told myself she was
exaggerating, that I couldn't think of much else. What with
having no book to write and Liz's letter, I saw that it was
time I moved on. I thought too that I'd better learn a bit
about Halliday, since he must be behind the whole
operation. I didn't like the reference to his *power*. I began to
have nightmares. They weren't really bad ones but
suffused with worry. I mean, in the diminished response
that you can have in a dream to events that in "real" life
would fill you with terror, it was worry I felt when my
dream self was condemned to be hanged, not the terror I
should have felt if it had been actual. For a man who
doesn't normally dream (no unconscious, as she used to
say) they were a turn-up for the book. It was a pity about
Kestrel and Emmy.

I packed my clothes, disposed of the load of post I'd
brought back from Titograd and went to Rome, wearing
my dark glasses. In the big city I tried to look Halliday up in
reference books. It was odd. I couldn't find him.
Admittedly I looked in the wrong book, I looked in *Who's
Who* when I should have looked in *Who's Who in America*,
but after all *Who's Who* has people like Fulbrights,
ambassadors, Secretaries of State and all that lot—but no
Halliday! I began to wonder and would have spent more
time in Rome had it not been for a condensation of the
thought that he was either not important enough or else
too bloody important to go in with the rest of us riff-raff
and a nightmare that *did* do more than worry me. It filled
me with dread. I dreamed I was in Rome, which is where I
was. I dreamed I saw one of those scrawled posters that
news boys and girls keep by them and up to date, as it
might be GUERRA? or something about a nun winning

102

a lottery, SBALIO! This one, however, was DOV'È BARCLAY? I hurried on in my dream and then, as I might well have done in "real" life, hurried back to assure myself that I hadn't been mistaken, but I couldn't find it and I woke up sweating.

I went right round the world. It's probably been done before—going round the world because you're scared I mean—but it felt like a first. The bloody man, if that is what he was, was everywhere, or his influence or his property or his men and women. In Hawaii I was sitting at a bar and a man at the other end of it said quite clearly that Halliday owned half the island. The light was dim and anyway I had my sunglasses on, so I was able to shift along and ask him which half and he laughed and said the better half. After I got upstairs to my room I began to wonder whether we had been talking about Halliday. The name seemed to flicker but then the trouble about going round the world because you're scared is you tend to drink a lot. Credit cards are a blessing but since Global and Tracker you have to be awfully careful about dates. I wasn't. I got into trouble, believe it or not, through crossing the international dateline and I *still* can't understand why. But who after all, other than an airline pilot, can understand the international dateline? At the time I remember making things worse by claiming that it was all the fault of Halliday. This contretemps was bad enough, though it blew my cover and made a radio item. It made the box too, though only a long shot of me disappearing round a corner with my panama pulled down over my face. What was worse was that only two days later I was walking through a village in a far chillier climate, no matter where. I walked through a village and came to with a dreadful start because one item of the washing hung out to dry had been a sweater with OLE ASHCAN on it. Then I knew for certain that the shock of my arrest, however temporary, had knocked me off-centre. Also, as I said, I had been drinking more than usual and the time before that village had got a bit fogged except for the two days just before it. I must say the additional shock of the sweater had a knock-on effect and I started drinking again just when I had practically stopped for those forty-eight hours and I don't remember what happened. A very nice and incurious young man from the embassy got me out of that. He understood completely my need to hide from Mr Halliday and Rick. He accepted a cheque for various things I seemed to need to pay, I don't now remember what they were, and he saw me to a plane.

Chapter X

Two changes later—the young man had been all against my driving a car for a bit—I was on a Greek island that in those days had remote places in it where the sanitation was primitive which I have come not to mind, preferring it to the marble and plastic and ceramic perfections where you meet so many people. I mean, these days in a so-called good hotel the men's room is practically a club. You don't know who you'll find yourself pissing next to. The island was—and now there's no need to conceal the fact, I remind myself—Lesbos or Lesvos according to whether you did or did not do Greek in the fifth. I thought solitude and a beach would be very good for recuperating from my arrest or arrests and all that drink. So I had myself driven clear across the island to a rundown hotel and a huge beach. (You wouldn't believe the road! Part of it was a dried-up watercourse and part a stretch of stones all the size of a cricket ball—girl's fist—and only useful for stoning crows.) One of the good things about Greece is that the standard wine is undrinkable. I'd been in Greece before and for an extended stay, as they say, like everyone else. I'd drunk myself into kidding myself that I liked retzina and then drunk myself out of that delusion again. Now I was saved from myself, so to speak, except for a soft Cretan red without any resin in it—Minos, I think it was called—and you could buy it in *galonia* which are earthenware jars done up in withy and you can keep one or more by you.

So I swam gently and sometimes I lay on my back with my eyes shut and enjoyed the feeling that I didn't know what they were writing and saying about *Horses at the Spring* and nobody knew where I was so I couldn't be told anyway and by now Mr Halliday and Rick had been reduced to getting their claws into other people. I was a bit uneasy about what people would be saying, since *Horses at the Spring* had what might be mistaken for True Love in it and people wouldn't wear that though I couldn't very well tell them it was there to put off Halliday. However, as they say, ignorance is bliss or calm at any rate. So I lay for days on my tum in shallow water, a mask over my face, a snorkel up by my earhole and watched the lovely nameless indifferent creatures with their colours and stillnesses and sudden darts and habit of being chums all together between meals. Once, I deduce (my one bit of underwater archaeology), there'd been a harbour at one end of the beach and it's still visible just under the surface, since in restful, geological terms, the island goes up and down like a yoyo. It's full of small, harmless fish—small because everything bigger has been eaten by the fishermen who now have to go out miles and miles before they can find anything. This sunken harbour—I think of it as *my* harbour—is not as exotic or exciting as the stuff you see on the Great Barrier Reef or at Eilat on the Red Sea, I know, having tried them both, but gentler, if the word isn't too silly. Also the rundown hotel has only about three tourists a year and otherwise is patronized by the occasional Greek who is trying to sell, it may be, those incredible pictures of young women being serenaded from gondolas and so on, or sometimes selling God knows what.

Well. After a timeless time I was flippering myself gently back towards the beach from the outer wall of my underwater harbour when my mask filled with water. That happens to us chaps with beards because you can't get enough spit on your moustache to make it waterproof. For some reason—I was in about nine inches—I knelt up and tore the thing off with a gesture of impatience. At that, a man who was bending down and adjusting his own mask, pushed it up on his forehead and gave a positive squeak.

"It can't be! Yes it is— Ho, I say, aren't I the lucky one!

106

You are Lobby Lubb and I claim the *News Chronicle* Award!"

"Go away, Johnny, go away. You're mistaken. Damn."

"I'd know that beard with the kind of incipient fork in it anywhere. Your face is going bald, my dear. You'll have to wear falsies, a toupée for the lower face. I can see it coming *in.*"

I sat up, holding my mask and snorkel. It was like the end of the holidays. I clasped my knees to my chest and looked at him glumly.

"Is it any good asking you to keep your mouth shut?"

Johnny wound his considerable length down into the water and sat in front of me.

"Well now, Wilf. That depends, doesn't it? As a matter of fact, I'm far too worried about mun to think of anything else—desperately short in fact. I wonder—"

"Yes, yes. The same as last time."

"That's jolly D. I must say, Wilf—"

"Skip it."

"Well, if you *won't* be bothered with thanks— What are you doing here?"

"If it comes to that, what are you?"

"Tit for tat—I'm not telling if you're not telling. But seriously, Wilf, that latest thing of yours, *Horses at the Spring*—"

"I don't want to hear. Damn it, why in hell can one guarantee hearing bad news even in a howling desert?"

"But it's so moving, dear! Quote, so human, unquote. Those two young things—and comical old Assby. He's not by any chance remotely founded on the unessential characteristics of yours truly? Otherwise how do you know so much, Wilf? After all, you've never thought yourself to be one of us, have you? Mixed, of course, withdrawn and shall we say in earliest days the wee-est bit experimental?"

"I don't want to hear about the bloody book."

Johnny straightened out and lay on his tum.

"Well," he said, quite unable to avoid a tiny infliction, "well, Wilf, I don't suppose you will after a bit."

I had my compulsions too.

"How bad was it, then?"

"Now, Wilf! Who said anything about it being bad? Believe me, in all sincerity, when the spring runs over and they silently realize their love, huge tears welled into my eyes. They *did!"*

He giggled. I waited for a while, then knelt up. Johnny saw he might miss some fun. He cried out.

"You simply can't go away, Wilf! You couldn't get a car over from the harbour before tomorrow and that's the sabbath, let alone the local saint's day, which you wouldn't miss on any account! The litany's gorgeous— 'God bless us and God bless them and to hell with the Turks.' General reaction wasn't too bad, I do assure you. Of course, we know the creatures that simply would do a knife job, don't we? Lilian and both the Henrys. The young creature on the box said it was *warm-hearted*, a thing he'd never thought to find himself saying of you. There! I've made your day, haven't I?"

"As bad as that. Well, who cares so long as the money's good?"

"Not you, dear, evidently. Even Lilian saying that when you tried to get warmth into a character it slopped all over the place is water off the duck's back!"

I fished round for something to say. I think I was trying to be honest.

"After all—you have to write the bad books if you're going to write the good ones."

"Work on that, Wilf. At present it sounds like a poor translation from the French. At least you were approved of by Emmy's young man."

"What Emmy?"

"Your Emmy. Yours and Liz's. The young man she went about with for a bit, that *vast* American academic—"

"Tucker! He's still in Europe?"

"I had quite a *tendre* for him for a while—at least a week. He's huge, isn't he? Do you think he could be persuaded to be cruel? But then the trouble with these large Americans,

108

they will keep on showering and using a positively asexual deodorant, unlike our local fishermen—have you sat down wind of them yet? It's enough to give one an orgasm."

"What was he doing with Emmy? I mean—where does he get his money from? He's married to— He had a sabbatical only four years ago—perhaps he's got the push. Goody goody."

"You don't know?"

"Know what?"

"That pretty little thing—"

"Helen—I mean, Mary Lou—"

"Right. Aha! So *that*'s where the warmth in *Horses at the Spring* comes from! Yes, she does have something, doesn't she? So unfair. Well. She's back in the States. Tucker has a line out to some philanthropist, a billionaire. She's got a job with him as a secretary or researcher or something. *Something*, I suppose."

"Halliday!"

"That's the name."

—and I was back in the Weisswald, sitting before the view of Mary Lou, truly inspirational.

No, Wilf. Mr Halliday is very fond of ladies.

Billions. Trillions. Mary Lou is interested in astronomy. Quadrillions. Money enough to start the Big Bang. Able to buy Mary Lou not with the lithe limbs of Paris. The girl you meet too late. The girl you have forgotten. That bit of you dissected out, a rare specimen. Able to buy Wilf, track him down, send forth. Run or stay still, in the end he'll get you. He can stand still and wait for you to arrive. Purchasable purity, sanctity, holiness, beauty incomparable. Oh grieve for her, that circle she had tried to complete with Rick, make him invulnerable, now seen to be brittle and irretrievably broken—

"Wilf?"

"You know, when the circle's broken and she's no longer looking inward but can look outward at somebody else she's probably quite different—probably a fascinating conversationalist and not physically heavy under the influence of his gravity but light as air, flirtatious—"

"You know? You're in fugue!"

"Halliday."

"I must say, Wilf—the sun is very strong, isn't it? Perhaps—"

"What do you know about Halliday?"

"It's time we got under cover."

Rick probably left him a note on some enormous bare executive desk, oh acres and acres of it in consideration of the services hereinafter specified of my wife Mary Lou Tucker—

"One billion, I should think."

"Come along, Wilf. Can't afford to lose you, can we?"

With that sort of money Rick could afford to have the CIA and the FBI and our own useless lot, let alone the KGB, on my track! It accounted for my justifiable unease in so many places, passports and all that.

"Off with our tiny flippers, Wilf, there's a dear."

"Bugger off, Johnny, if you're capable of it."

"Now that was horrid."

"I mean it."

"I must say, Wilf, apart from my unnatural affection for you, you intrigue me. Why a man ostensibly so indifferent to society should be, if I may coin a phrase, so shit-scared of critical opinion—"

"Well. Aren't you critical opinion, and if so can you wonder?"

"Rudesby!"

Clearly Halliday was more dangerous than Rick. After all, with his sources of information he didn't have to guess. He simply knew my biography and could pass it on to that hairy hack Rick Tucker.

"*Who* knows your biography?"

Johnny was standing on the front step of the hotel. He had stopped pulling me by the wrist, though he still had hold of it and he was staring into my face. I shook off his hand.

110

"Got to shower."

"The water won't be on yet, as well you know."

"Got to lie down."

Johnny nodded seriously.

"That's—er, the ticket. Great nature's second course. *Macbeth*, q.v."

"Ha et cetera."

Johnny was still nodding to himself when I got myself away from him.

I was tired from swimming and knew that any clothes I put on would be sticky from salt and then sweat. I sat on the edge of my bed and determined to do nothing. I did not move, I hardly breathed. I did not think or feel. I willed myself into a state of nothingness, of deliberate catatonia like a limpet that the tide has left. I came to out of that state with an anguished click!—perhaps it was audible—like a blind running up and letting in cruel daylight. I was remembering Prescott. I never knew the man himself only his letters and the manuscript he kept plaguing me with. It was bad, hopelessly bad, though there was a good idea buried in it. I told him all that, yet he kept plaguing me for years with requests and ideas. At last I had to ignore him. But the thing was that the central idea in my fourth novel *was exactly the good one hidden in Prescott's awful manuscript!* Of course, it was properly treated and all that, but still! I swear that when writing *The Endless Plain* and ever since I had not even thought of Prescott or the manuscript or the whole trying non-association which is only too familiar in type to any writer once he has got out before the public.

Had I remembered? Was it wholly the work of the unconscious that Liz didn't believe I suffered from, or had I stolen the idea deliberately at some point? As far as I knew, Prescott had never succeeded in publishing the MS he sent me, though by now he had enough books to his name and was probably as well known as I am. Would he remember and make a point of it in some interview? It seemed to me, as the afternoon turned into a somewhat cooler evening, that there was not a single absurd, humiliating or quasi-criminal act in my life that did not come back to sting and burn me.

When at last I went downstairs, since there was only the one hotel in the place it was inevitable Johnny should be waiting for me.

"Ouzo, Wilf, to take the look of anguish off your face."

"God forbid. I keep my own *galoni* in the bar. It's drinkable. Minos."

"I must say, my dear, it can only be those famous wanderings of yours that keep your figure even reasonably within bounds the way you positively *rape* the bottle."

"Famous?"

"You and Ambrose Bierce. Quote, where is Wilfred Barclay whose recent novel *Horses at the Spring*, unquote."

"Oh shut up. If it comes to that, what are you writing yourself?"

"Little me? A huge picture book for the rainbow people. About Sappho, of course. I'm undecided whether to call it *Ladies of Lesvos* or *Burning Sappho*. I wish someone had really burned the wretched girl. There's nothing known about her, nothing at all. Besides it's nominally history and I'm not feeling creative."

"That your best one-liner to date."

"Funny or not, whenever I turn to the thing I get in such a pet!"

"You're not a classical scholar."

"I'm an erotic scholar. You wouldn't believe the information I've managed to amass from my women chums, to say nothing of guesswork. You'll swear, I know, not to pinch the idea, but what do you suppose neolithic ladies used those dinky little carvings of the earth mother for? I've even embarked on bogus philology—rather like canting heraldry—and claim that 'Lesbos' is derived from 'Olisbos', classical Greek for what the ads call a Sex Aid. How do you get on in your wanderings, Wilf? Still in the missionary position?"

"How do you?"

"One doesn't ask for permanence."

He fell silent and during that silence I drifted off into a dreary brood only to surface when I heard Johnny speak again.

"*Why* are you deadly sick of all this?"

He was eager again and scanning the various visible areas of my face for information. It came to me that his next move would be to tell Rick where I was. Come to that, he could sell the information to the press or any or all of the bloody media.

"Where is he now?"

"Who, Wilf?"

"My—my would-be biographer."

"Aren't you the lucky thing? Displaying one's all! Nobody has offered to write my life, alas. I shall have to do it myself, such a thankless task, a sort of literary masturbation which, say what you will—"

"In my case—"

"Yes, yes, I know. You are about to proclaim your *complete* heterosexuality like silly young Keats. Do you remember? I think it's in 'Lamia'. Dear, dear Wilf! You must have it as an epigraph for your Collected Works. Let me see—yes.

> Let the mad poets say whate'er they please
>   Of the sweets of Faeries, Peris, Goddesses,
> There is not such a treat among them all,
>   Haunters of cavern, lake and waterfall,
> As a real woman—

What a vulgarian! One can see why it got itself called the 'Cockney School'."

My *galoni* had appeared and I started drinking. Those memories were like worms eating into the flesh, Jake pursuing, worms eating, and monstrous Halliday brooding over all. I thought to myself that the strain was building up in me because I'd stopped writing and should instantly start on another book, but the trouble was my head was empty of all but these thoughts triggered by John

St John John who was continuing to talk whether I listened or not.

"Beware of the worm—"

I came to with a dreadful start. *He* had said that, not I! Of course, I've worked out since then that while I was brooding in what I thought was silence I must have muttered something about the worm; but at the time it was terrifying as necromancy. It seemed to me that everyone in the world but I could see, had some sort of access, and only I was trapped in myself, ignorant, bounded by my own skin with none of the antennae *They* seemed to have in order to reach out and touch my secret self.

"What worm?"

"—that flies in the night in the howling storm—wasn't Britten divinely *clever*? I do envy composers, don't you? Like mathematicians. They don't have to have any politics and that sort of thing, just sit up there on a cloud."

"What worm?"

"My dear boy. They are eating you alive. Shall I give you a complete diagnosis?"

"No."

"You see, you are what biologists used to call exoskeletal. Most people are what they called endoskeletal, have their bones inside. But you, my dear, for some reason known only to God, as they say of anonymous bodies, have spent your life inventing a skeleton on the outside. Like crabs and lobsters. That's terrible, you see, because the worms get inside and, oh my aunt Jemima, they have the place to themselves. So my advice, seeing you're going to make me a loan and *noblesse oblige* et cetera, is to get rid of the armour, the exoskeleton, the carapace, before it's too late."

"Any suggestions?"

"You could try, let me see, religion, sex, adoption, good works—I think sex is the best in the circumstances. After all, even lobsters get together, though I must confess I don't see how, quite. It's probably the extraordinary onanism that One Above allows to go on unblasted provided it's under water."

"Salmon and suchlike."

"Just so. You've been reading that little verse I wrote for the *TLS*. 'For man is a funniful fish, a mere fish but a queer fish, a holy roly poly fish, very particular where his milt (the queerest flesh of the fish) is spilt.' And so on. Good, don't you think?"

"No."

"Curse you. A *jeu d'esprit*, of course. You have no sense of rhythm, I've always thought so."

"I'm tired."

"As I was saying, you need a chum. You see, my dear, I know a thing or two. You think I'm an ageing queer in your categorizing way, and of course I am, among other things. I don't think I'll try the snail soup. It'll have to be mousaka again. Isn't Greek food perfectly loathsome? If it weren't for bloody Sappho— At the very *least* you need a woman. Or are you the sort who discovers himself late in life and goes overboard for some handsome young fellow?"

"Oh for God's sake, shut up!"

"All that must have gone from you, drifted away into the far beyond, yes, my dear, gone from you in the battle and strife. Yes. You need a woman."

"Have you anyone in mind?"

"Therein the patient et cetera."

"*Macbeth*, q.v."

"Do you know what Apollo said? Well, of course you do! Know thyself. Perhaps you've gone all these years without knowing yourself at all. You need a chum. Start at the bottom with a dog."

"I don't like them."

"Worms under the carapace isn't just human sadism, you see. It's the pure poetry of the art. Only One Above could be as inventive as that."

"I'm tired of talking of Halliday. I mean—"

"Ah well. You always were a prose person, weren't you?"

115

"With wit."

"And where has your celebrated 'callous wit' gone, *je me demande?*"

"I'm old. I'm going faster and faster—"

"Where?"

I think I must have shouted.

"Where we're all going, you bloody fool!"

I *think* I can remember what he said after that word for word, because I have a very clear picture of his face coming closer to mine across the little dinner table, so close I could see he had pencilled his eyebrows.

"Wilf, dear. Once more in return for the loan. See a priest or a shrink. If not, at least keep away from doctors acting in tandem. Otherwise they'll have you inside before you can say 'dipso-schizo'."

Chapter XI

This isn't a biography. I don't quite know what it is, since there are enormous gaps where I don't remember what happened and other gaps because I remember that nothing happened. If all that wasn't bad enough in the attempt to get some kind of coherence into this mass of paper, the months after Lesvos and Johnny are patchy because of the state I was in. I remember seeing clearly, that same night after Johnny had done his ridiculous diagnosis, that I must get away at all costs. But instead I got sodden, moving in a haze of Minos from day to day and seeing little of Johnny, who didn't number excessive drinking among his several vices. At last I did manage to get myself transported to the airstrip and flew off. (Forwarding address: Rinderpest, Bloemfontein, SA.) Thank God for planes! They can alter the whole outlook in the merest fraction of time like at the Last Trumpet. I remember sitting next to some chap, a Canadian I think, and maundering on about how marvellous flying was because if you flew enough you were bound to crash, and if you crashed in a jet death was instantaneous, much to be desired, *Julius Caesar*, q.v. This Canadian was what Johnny would call a cowardy cowardy custard and did not like to be reminded that we were suspended by a crazy application of the laws of aerodynamics over a lot of nasty deep water. He went and changed his seat. Well, I knew Athens would be stuffed with chaps from Great Britain or the States, so I simply changed planes and flew to South Africa, forgetting that South Africa was what I had given as a forwarding address. I remembered that on the way there and determined to come back by return. But—and here the patchiness comes in—I got into a nursing home somehow. I'd had a vivid encounter with the red hot worms under my carapace and a nice female doctor got them out of me through various chinks which she demonstrated by showing me a live lobster from the fish market and then again sometimes I think I dreamed the whole thing. Of course, she left the heat inside me but I thought I could put up with that. I felt that a milder climate would make the heat bearable perhaps but what with one forwarding address and another I was running short of countries where I'd not been compromised. So I flew to Rome (forwarding address: Shangri La, Katmandu, Nepal) and no sooner had we landed than I remembered Rick in the Piazza Navona. So I doubled back on my tracks, taking a local flight with a hire car at the end of it. I drove off very slowly for I hadn't made much of a fist at signing my name to the thing you sign.

Now I have to tell you about that island although I don't want to, it still gives me the jitters. But I have to tell about the island because it's the first half. I'll write the second half later. As a matter of fact I've been screwing myself up to do it for some time and I can't do it sober, that's the fact of the matter. Oh I know in the morning I'll be going down to the kitchen to count the empties with no Liz to glide in like the ghost of something in *Vogue*. No Rick to go through the dustbin, the ole ashcan. He's probably wandering about outside somewhere to keep an eye on me. Since Liz had the ashes cut down I can look straight across the lawn from where I'm sitting to the woods on the other side of the river or I would if I could but I am not able, it being about three o'clock in some morning. That's where the badgers come from to badger me and Rick too.

Well. I got one ferry and landed up in the city where they incontinently shot the chief of police in the main street before my very eyes. It was the Mafia and I had some sort of idea that Halliday was using them so I took another ferry. I don't mean back to where I'd come from but onward, ever onward, and found myself with car on a

118

quay whence the streets were too narrow to drive along. So as I didn't much like the look of the combined slum, hovel, bar, knocking shop they called the hotel Marina, I walked off into the town, to find something bigger and better with a decent bar instead of a plank held up by two ancient slatterns. I came to a gate, opened it and walked to some houses which seemed to suggest they might conceal one of those Italian villas that always get turned into hotels. I should have noticed that these houses didn't have windows. Silly of me. Well, I walked into a kind of long corridor in one and of course they had ancient corpses all dressed up and standing against the wall for support, you couldn't expect them to stand up without, I mean. I was shaking when I got out of there but the odd thing about these shakes was that when they should have stopped because I was no longer more frightened than usual the shaking went on. I stopped there among the windowless houses and shouted at them.

"The island's shaking!"

So it was, too. Telling the living or the dead about shakes in that island was taking coals to Newcastle and no mistake. Well, I did find a hotel with windows and no visible corpses except the barman who hadn't been used for years and they fetched my bag from the car and I sat up all night on the side of the bed waiting for the shaking to stop but it didn't. I must have slept, but the thing was that either I'd invented an unconscious or had had one all along despite what Liz said and I dreamed, my God how I dreamed! I must have had breakfast because I remember wandering about and seeing that the island consisted of powdered pumice with knives of black glass sticking up through it like a feast of steeples. An interesting place for normal people but not for you if you are creaky on the hinge. I suppose it *was* there? Yes, of course it was because of what came after.

At some point I decided I would stick to coffee and I spent the morning with buckets of it. Then to keep myself sober I decided to go for a walk, avoiding the *centre ville*, the dead centre, ha et cetera. Sicilian burial customs, q.v.

So out I went, cautiously hugging the walls. There was a big hill and I began to stalk it. Yes, I know quite well it sounds crazy; but then, it was. I began to approach it as if the old man himself, I mean my contemporary, according to Mary Lou—why, he's no older than you are! What a liar the girl is. I was deceived in her. He is older than the church on which he shits. Pretty squalid the streets were, even for that area, I can tell you. I saw soon that the building that came into sight on the top was a church, probably a cathedral; and feeling so hot inside I thought I would case the cool joint for glass though the chance of anything other than atrocious stuff presented by the Mafia in about 1900 was minimal. After a time I had to stop, being out of puff, but no matter how long I waited I could feel the heat inside me and the heat outside me for the day was sweltering. It wasn't ordinary daylight, it was incandescent daylight, not sunlight at all but an atmosphere with a luminescence in it. I thought at first it might be the drink but then realized if I could think that I wasn't as bad with drink as I'd thought but with the other thing—being chased, I mean, and spied on, that not to put too fine a point on it was unbalancing my judgement just a little. As far as booze was concerned I hadn't a trace of hangover which is a bad sign. Even the circle of sea round the island had an odd, brassy look about it. There was an islander coming down the hill past me and he was crossing himself like a mechanical doll. *Then* I saw what was up and why the island had the shakes. At a point on the horizon, God knows what the direction was, there was the plume of black smoke like you'd get from a megaton.

You can say what you like but the earth shaking is worse than the shakes. It destroys the last little bit of human security, I mean the feeling that in the last analysis your feet have something solid to stand on. But the earth shaking is a reminder of the crazy ball flying through space which if you care or have to think of it is an enormity verging on, no, surpassing outrage. Nevertheless, if

120

you're looking for a description of the horrors of an eruption or earthquake you won't find it here because as I now see I was too far gone to do anything but accept the whole thing as a personal insult or tribute and anyway the shakes—I mean the earth shakes—died away: and of course when I came out of that place on top of the hill I couldn't have cared if the whole island, glass knives and all, had sunk into the sea.

There was a vast ascent of steps, vast not only in extent—they seemed to go straight up to the sky—but vast in width. You could have marched a company up them in line abreast, and very appropriate, for they were donkey steps, the rise small, the step wide as wide, or perhaps the correct architectural term would be deep as deep. So up I went, brother ass protesting for all that he had these specially constructed steps for his convenience, until I reached the flat space in front of the main door of the huge building. It was the west door and it's just possible I suppose that what happened after that couldn't have happened in any other place but who can tell? There was an ancient lady sitting outside the central door of three on a rush chair and spinning a fine thread. *No*, she wasn't one of the Fates, she was an ancient lady put there to see that none of the tourists who visited the place every ten years or so had a camera with him. Why? They don't like pics and very right and proper too. It was a change to find people who know as I do that a pic takes something away from you, so I spoke my best broken Italian to her, assuring her that I wasn't the sort of man to carry a *machina photographica* round with me. But she quite clearly didn't understand, speaking nothing but whatever it is they speak in the island. However to show willing I pointed at the plume of smoke on the horizon and raised my eyebrows, whereat she started crossing herself, all rhythm of spinning interrupted.

"Volcano!"

She knew that word all right. Well, at least it wasn't the bomb. A pretty place I've been led to, I thought to myself, it's ho for those homely motor roads, Wilf, when the ferry comes back and be damned to Rick and Halliday and their Mafia. So in I went and it was very, very dark, even for a church.

That was when I realized I still had my outsize sunglasses on; and I inferred from that they'd been in position for some days even when sitting on the side of the bed, or possibly dreaming. It was odd, standing inside the kind of preliminary wooden box between the inner and outer door to consider that it also implied I hadn't washed for some time. So I took them off, pushed open the inner door and sidled in.

It was a cathedral all right because I could see the cathedra. I took a step or two forward, glancing round and I saw at once that the glass wasn't worth a second glance. I went forward a bit more, noting that the roof was the best bit as the spandrels were full of quite early mosaic. Mosaic is like glass—the earlier the better. I took a step or two forward, thinking that I'd case the joint quickly then concentrate on the good bits, when a piece of mosaic fell at my feet with the day's last shake.

Now. I had been advancing slowly. That tiny fragment of dirty blue stone fell a yard in front of me and I stood on my right foot, about to put the left one down but I kept it there in the air and looked at the stone. It was less than half an inch square. It lay directly in front of me. I put down my left foot and stood. Mountains throw cannon balls at me, churches drop a bit of stone the size of a finger nail. Well, I thought, remembering what had happened because I didn't take any notice of the mountain's warning, we'd better go carefully here. You don't want to fall off the edge. What is more, there was something about that cathedral, an atmosphere. It was, now I saw in the absence of sunglasses, still darker than it had any right to be, seeing that the sun was brassy outside and most of the windows stark plain. You could call it a complete absence of gentle Jesus meek and mild. I didn't like it and was in half a mind to leave but knew that if I did I should only find myself in an endless stream of time with nothing to help me forget it. I went on.

How long did all that last? I sat on the surround of a pillar for a bit and was hot inside by contrast with the church's coolth. I had a strain inside my chest like being held up on tiptoe. The strain made sitting down to rest quite, quite pointless, so despite the bit of mosaic that had fallen in front of me, I went on.

It was in the north transept. It faced me across the whole width. It was a solid silver statue of Christ but somehow the silver looked like steel, had that frightening suggestion of blue. It was taller than I am, broad-shouldered and striding forward like an archaic Greek statue. It was crowned and its eyes were rubies or garnets or carbuncles or plain red glass that flared like the heat in my chest. Perhaps it was Christ. Perhaps they had inherited it in these parts and just changed the name and it was Pluto, the god of the Underworld, Hades, striding forward. I stood there with my mouth open and the flesh crawling over my body. I knew in one destroying instant that all my adult life I had believed in God and this knowledge was a vision of God. Fright entered the very marrow of my bones. Surrounded, swamped, confounded, all but destroyed, adrift in the universal intolerance, mouth open, screaming, bepissed and beshitten, I knew my maker and I fell down.

I believe it was the fat woman who had been spinning outside the door who found me. She wouldn't have heard my screams, I think, not in that place. She wouldn't have listened anyway, having her ears pricked for a belly rumble from the other island. But there must have come a time when she did her rounds of the place, checking perhaps that I hadn't run off with the church plate. So she must have found me.

I came to in hospital and didn't even have to begin remembering. I came to with the memory. I lay, watched by a nun who told her beads just the way the old lady had spun. I don't know if it's normal to have a nun watch you.

It may be that since I'd been struck down in the cathedral they thought they had a special responsibility for me or something. I don't know and of course it doesn't matter. I don't think the hospital was very good.

I lay for—oh, for a long, long time. I saw so many things with great clarity as if the light of the previous day, if it was the previous day, had filled me with its dreadful luminescence. I could not think anything or see anything but the truth. I saw that I had been planned from the beginning. I had my place in things. It didn't matter what I had done or would do. I had been created by that ghastly intolerance in its own image. You may possibly recognize what I am talking about though it would be better for you if you did not. I saw I was one of the, or perhaps the only, predestinate damned. I saw this hotly and clearly. In hell there are no eyelids.

A priest came and mumbled and I laughed which annoyed him and set the nun crossing herself as if steam-driven. The joke that I saw so clearly was this. The priest wasn't a priest at all because all the real priests of the intolerance had been dead for thousands of years and he was like someone in a stage set. He went away, perhaps to take off his make-up. The doctor came after the priest and he was a bit better. He held both my hands and squeezed them, nodding. I understood that he wanted me to squeeze back, which I did. He went all over me and he said a word, frowning. When he saw I couldn't understand he used another.

"Colpo. Colpo?"

Mea maxima culpa. Ha et cetera. I thought I knew what he meant and tried to speak, "Si, massima colpa," but I couldn't get it out, there was an ox on my tongue. He did a whole lot of smiling and nodding and patting, then went away. When he came back in the evening he had some new words.

"Estrook. Piccolo. Leedle estrook."

That made me laugh again, thinking of the universal flail, but the doctor only went on nodding and smiling and testing my reflexes, the result of which tests, he persuaded me, added up to a tiny stroke though I could have told him drunks like me don't have strokes, they get the horrors of one sort or another and now and then come across a real beauty, first prize, predestined and damned, the divine justice without mercy. *In vino veritas,* my other tag.

The memory of it all still makes me hot. At half-past three in the morning it has made me a contemplative, stone-cold sober. I mean contemplative in the technical sense, contemplating a universal reality. They say some strokes—well, there's no "they say" about it, I know from experience that some leedle estrooks make you speak one word when you mean another. They say too that there's no rime or reason about the relationship between the two words, no connection except the nature of the physical brain but I know better. Wilfred Barclay, the great consultant. There is every connection as for example saying "dead" when you mean "dad" and "mare" when you mean "mum". It—apart from the steel hard *factuality* of the intolerance—is what makes me know it wasn't a leedle estrook at all, or if it was, the event was no more than coincidental.

What does it matter? Lying in that hard bed, unnunned, blessedly ignored and allowed to contemplate the nature of predestinate insects or, moving up-market, lobsters and crabs, crusty chaps; looking for the primordial moment of will, our will I mean, and not finding it, knowing that we did not, I repeat did not, invent ourselves and that now in this eternal fix it is not what we do that will help, it is what we are that matters and what we are is not in our hands; lying, I say with the insolence of the damned who have nothing to lose and therefore do not have to suck up in a pointless attempt at influencing divine intolerance, a steel Hades, striding forward! Lying there, I say, either the verbal transpositions of my leedle estrook or it may be my natural language composed quite spontaneously a kind of set of psalms, antipsalms if you like, the natural blasphemy of our condition, why this is hell nor am I out of

125

it, Marlowe, q.v. It is like the spontaneous effort by which a certain kind of wasp will lay eggs in a certain caterpillar it all makes good sense you wouldn't expect anything else. What irony that it should have been so reasonable, so sane! Because during that time I must have *seemed* wholly mad with garbled speech, mumbling to myself in a language which wasn't even English *but my native tongue*.

However, I survived that state and began attempts to relearn a foreign language, the one I am using now. For a time I stuck to single syllables and it was quite interesting or would have been had I not still had the strain inside me, tuning me up, I thought, like a steel violin string—would I were catgut to snap and be done with, that's what I thought, having early in life recognized that ninety-nine per cent of this language is metaphor and now having suspicions about the odd one per cent. Anyway I practised this foreign language to take the place of my so-called mumbles. It was difficult. It was like moving each syllable from here to there no that won't do it was like having laboriously to refashion a statue, paint a complex picture, not to say "liquor" with your mouth when your mind had thought "sunrise". I walked through the hospital regulations in a state *cognate* that's the right word to madness or delirious trimmings which since by your time the whole load of religious stuff will have come back with a bang or with the bang or bangs I've lost my thread.

At some point I found myself back in the hotel, then in the hire car, then in the ferry, each of these stages being quite separate like pictures in frames, and not very important compared with the violin string being wound tighter and tighter the note shriller and old nobodaddy there everywhere. But I went on practising my single syllables in its despite. On that ferry (I was watching an Italian cruise ship I think the Italians said she was the *Cristoforo Colombo* so for my biography I mean our biography you can find the exact place and date) I tried with my mind to think the word "end". I spoke it out loud and what my mouth said was "sin". This made me laugh in a lopsided way as I considered the relationship between this new word, the heat in my body, the steel string, the vision, all those things a biography would uncover that I had tried to cover in our dance. Oh it made me laugh all right. But at least I now had the alchemy of one word and might add others. It was like walking on thin ice.

"My—sin."

I got that out all right. But of course it was the old intolerance's deliberate mistake that has made calamity of so much. I tried again, not being minded to be its fool.

"Not. Sin. I. am. sin."

Chapter XII

I haven't the heart or courage to reread that lot. It was a bad time and the very memory tempts me to the bottle which I am anxious to avoid. Behold old Filthy Rags wandering with the immediate awareness that old you-know-who has its eye on him no matter what. I didn't mind the wanderings much because there was nothing to be done. I can't explain that, you'll have to take it as read. There was nothing to be done. *Please* see the joke! Here was Wilfred Barclay with the world willing (in a small way) to beat a path to his door (not at home). Here was old Wilf with what young men long for, as much money as he could spend and more, growing old, of course, but not aware he was screaming, dismarried if I can put it that way and quite possibly some sort of marriageable commodity if he had stayed long enough in one place, able to ride, fly, glide, sit, stand, walk, healthy in mind and body against all the odds with the world wide open for him—here, I say, was Wilf in a state of perfect freedom. People should be warned against it. Freedom should carry a government health warning like cancer sticks! Teach that in the schools, thunder it from the pulpits, rise to propose it, Mr Speaker, hear hear, at all costs do not trust it, gentle maiden!

Is that what I am trying to convey?

Well. There is freedom and freedom. Surfacing as I say, I dissected myself into various portions that were at once held together and threatened by the steel string. The first thing I tried was catatonia. That provided a straightforward blow to the Barclay pride. I couldn't keep it up. I couldn't pretend I wasn't. The loo, for one thing. Adepts in the kingdom of Catatonia are able to ignore that

128

as well so their obedient slaves do them up in nappies or what Rick would call diapers. I just wasn't good enough at it, that's all. Despite my every wish (and here you see the wilder shores of freedom receding) I'd have to get up and go to the loo. I even had to eat and drink, not booze, I mean but water, tea, coffee, limejuice, wet stuff. I couldn't even avoid the thought that girls were interesting. Well, not interesting, just a lot of other things. I discovered my dreadful hatred for homosexuality. When it came to the point that I could recognize catatonia was a dead loss I thought I'd try fun. Fun. That's what I thought. Be your age, I said, you're only in your sixties after all and you can go on facing your youth, you don't have to look behind you except every now and then. Commit. That verb is to remain intransitive. Go forth old man and commit. Commit afresh. Since there's nothing to be done you might as well do something. Have some fun, hon. That set me to considering the deepest double-dyed commit that I could find. Now I, being a true Christian child of the twentieth century, you will think that I evolved some funny stuff with girls or children; but not so.

This commit. It made me laugh at the time though not now of course, not after what has happened since and being where I am. There's the faintest light of dawn behind the woods across the river. Soon there'll be the dawn chorus though I shan't hear it over the clatter of this wretched machine. I ought to get a silent one and have left silent machines here and there, it was always simpler to get a new machine wherever I was than lug one round with me.

Well. Again, this commit. I came to the conclusion that the deed most in step with my newly discovered nature would be to kill Johnny's dog. Well. My dog, if you like. (Yes, I know you'll have forgotten Johnny's dog. Look it up.)

I went on thinking. I saw that a straightforward murder was childish stuff and unworthy of us both, unworthy of image and original. What was needed was something

129

philosophically, or rather theologically, *witty*. Believe me, I thought so long and hard that at times I might well have really been on the verge of catatonia! Moreover, the conclusion wasn't a dull, elaborate deduction like a scientific discovery so called that is the result of statistical compilation, it was a revelation. It opened out in sheer vistas that had me breathless with adoration like a nun. Wordsworth, q.v.

It was very difficult to find Rick. I was in some country or other, Portugal I think or perhaps not, and I did it all by telephone. I got hold of my agent and my publishers. Of course, Rick had been on at them both but even so they didn't know where he was currently as they all said, only where he had been. For a time we must have kept the satellites buzzing. This surprised me because I thought he would be shackled by one leg to his university but not so. According to my agent he was loose, having been staked to do his research on yours truly and I didn't need telling to know that Halliday must have staked him. I gave my agent a poste restante in Rome and went there, no longer wanting to avoid Rick but rather having a definite need of him to complete things. They must have rung round in England too because at the poste restante I got a ton of stuff from my publishers, from my agent, from Liz and rubbish from God knows where. I got a taxi and took it back to the sleazy hotel by La Rotonda in sacks.

It was far too much to examine in detail so I left it strewn round the place, rang my agent and actually gave him my telephone number and the name of the hotel I was staying at! I'd got beyond any bother about blowing my cover. He came back within the hour with a message from my publishers who did now *know* where Rick was. He was lecturing on guess who or what in Hamburg University. I already had my plans laid so I drove straight off, heading north for Switzerland. When I had got far enough away from Rome I stopped and rang him from one of those mini markets attached to gas stations and I got him in ten seconds flat, which is remarkable even in these days of instant everything. He hadn't caught up with me in years, despite all those near misses. When I thought of the number of times I'd *seen* him or *remembered* seeing him nosing about on my trail I laughed aloud at the thought of my voice coming to him out of the blue.

"Where are you, Wilf, where are you? Hold on! Don't go!"

"I won't."

"But you've done it so often and then just hung up!"

"Don't be wet!"

"Where are you then?"

"Let's just say I'm on a motor road."

"Yurp or the States?"

"A motor road. Now listen, Rick old friend. I want to see you."

"Well, surely, surely! God! It is really you?"

"I'm going to meet you in a place we both know."

"Any place, Wilf! My God!"

"That hotel in the Weisswald."

Then there was a long, long silence. Even the girl at the till thought I'd finished and looked up. I wondered if I'd spoiled things.

"I'm waiting, Rick."

"Well, I know, Wilf."

I decided it was time to sprinkle a little bait.

"I've been thinking about the biography, Rick."

"Oh my God, Wilf, it's like being—like being saved by the bell. My God! He gave me seven years and—"

"I'll be there Thursday. Get your Mr Halliday to buy you the ticket right now.

"Hell, the Weisswald isn't far. I can make it without."

"How's it with Mary Lou, Rick?"

There was a pause. My mind's eye saw his chin sink back. Not a good phoner, our Rick. His voice came over low and defensive.

"They have a beautiful relationship, Wilf."

"Like us."

There was a period of white sound. I carried on.

131

"I'll be there on Thursday. Don't turn up till Saturday. I want to live myself in. Acclimate."

I hung up. I'm not like Rick, I find it easy to be firm on the phone—easier than face to face. It's as if my faceless voice is a different person I can use the way some people use a solicitor to say their dirty work for them. So on I drove with the tight wire in my chest and on and on. I spent a night, I remember, in that colossal motel wherever it is, then over the mountains and far away to the dear old Weisswald. I didn't seem to mind the rack railway so much this time, it was odd. I was welcomed to the hotel not by Herr Adolf Kaufmann whose recommendation is included somewhere in this opus but by his nephew, an entirely different Adolf Kaufmann, who having consulted the hotel filing system greeted me as an old friend and gave me the familiar suite with a bottle of Dôle already opened on the table. And they say that values are not what they were! It was odd to find the manager so much younger though. The fat woman had died and the décor of the bar was changed, that was all. It sent me to the bathroom mirror to look at myself and, my God, I saw myself for the first time in years and years. If you don't change your hairstyle because it's mostly fallen out and you don't shave, you've no cause to go chasing yourself in a mirror. Yes, time had done some engraving over most of what was visible and I reminded myself to go back to washing regularly. I made a clever deduction from this and had a shower at once. My bag didn't seem to have any underclothes in it so I sent out for some which arrived promptly.

I forgot to say that there was a photograph hanging in the bar. I looked at it idly enough at first. It was the sort of photograph you see in the cheaper glossies, Commander W. F. "Gutsy" Hunkelberry-Fawcett sitting this one out with a young friend at Fartmouth Hunt Ball—

Then I saw that the waiter was the manager's uncle, old Kaufmann deceased. This led me to a consideration of the bearded oaf sitting at the table and grinning clownishly across it at the wench on the other side. Yes of course, our sins shall find us out, there's One Above with a note book and a camera and he doesn't allow us to pose but simply snatches the pic at his own sweet will and at our disadvantage. It was Wilfred Barclay all right, famous Wilf, who thus conferred such distinction on the bar that they hung him there—taken at a moment when sitting down he couldn't fall down drunk; taken by his old chum, meaty Rick L. Tucker, the hairy Ainu, the strong man with his warmth and his deodorant and his bulging flies—why was there no photograph of *them*? They would do credit to any establishment. The flies, I mean.

And the girl. Yes, the girl. That's the thing about a flash. It blasts the life and colour out of a face, however delicate, so that this was not so much the Mary Lou who had adored her big strong man and tried as far as she could to complete the magic circle—oh no! This was the doll, the fashion model, the plastic imitation of a girl, white-faced, black-haired, the cloud of it frozen, the gentleness gone, destroyed. And yet they tell you that a camera does not tell the truth! There we were, Wilf the clown, still libidinous half a generation after he should have known better; and the girl, her lipstick black as her hair, her dumb, flat face an exact expression of that mind as interesting as a piece of string! I shut my eyes, unable to go on looking at the thing.

Even so, the oaf in the photograph was not as repellent as the man I had examined in my mirror. *That* would have made a photograph and a half! And Mary Lou, what had the years of failed marriage, the years of Halliday, done to her? Rick ought to take a photograph of us all over again, I thought, before and after, but of course it was like Lucinda, there are circumstances where you can't get the two faces you want on to the same pic, can't possibly get them there. So I went back, put on a change of underwear, confirmed that I couldn't buy a suit off the hook in Weisswald, wrenched open the french windows in "my" sitting-room, glanced at the Spurli, took a deep breath, strode across the balcony, seized the rail with both hands, bent over and looked down.

It was what commonly passes as hell for about five seconds. Then it was nothing but a quantity of space with a smash at the bottom, which was even a bit comforting. So I informed myself.

"You've come of age."

And, we'll agree, about time! I went back into the sitting-room, closing the french windows behind me. The table in the centre was still polished as if the ghost of the fat woman had been at work but probably it was only another fat woman. The only paper on it was a menu, lying beside the open bottle of Dôle. I looked at the bottle warily. It was going to be no good Rick finding me knocked out by booze and having the shakes. If I was going to be master, I reasoned, I had to muster every bit of firmness I could find in me. I out-stared the bottle—not as easy as you might think—then went looking for warm clothing. The manager fixed me up with a sweater and an anorak that had been left by visitors. It's astonishing what the kind of drunken louts who live for *après ski* will leave behind them. My sweater had TRY ME knitted into the front, like Rick's OLE ASHCAN. I set off with great care (remembering the way you have to acclimate) to walk the time away before I could reasonably allow myself a drink. Drink *does* slacken the steel string a bit but, as I've said or as you may have inferred, invariably leads to problems. It's no good relying on experience. Problems get worse with age, not better. If only I had a young head on old shoulders, ha et cetera. I went up along a chilly path from which the snow had only lately receded. It was the one which we had walked together years before and down which Rick had carried me. I should not have recognized it with snow lying all about except for the direction. Most of the scene I had never even glimpsed before because of the fog; but now everything was clear, as outer space. But it's true the old infirmity which had been called the need to acclimate came over me. I went on slower and slower and stopped. I didn't look about me much but sat down on a convenient outcrop

134

or jut of rock and waited for my heart and breath to get a bit easier. I found myself listening to the sound of water. It had only one voice, and this was the light, babbling one. I opened my eyes and when I looked down, believe it or not, I recognized the rock I was sitting on and there in front of me was the rail. Come to that, there was the stream. It was different of course, much broader for one thing and coming out of a snow bank from a cave of ice. This cave more or less squeezed the water flat, which was why it only had that top voice.

I looked round. My jaw must have fallen right down to my chest. I couldn't be mistaken. There, flooded, were those half trunks that had been made into conduits and sunk in the path. The stone was clinching evidence. It was too big to be moved without explosives or gangs and machines. It stuck out of the mountainside and had done so for geological time, I was certain. And yes, of course, the last time we had been there I had heard cowbells in the fog without having the wit to see what it meant. Old Quixote on the wooden horse.

Who was it, I thought, had set about designing something theologically witty? In about ten seconds I was near enough blind with humiliation and rage—not at once rage with Rick; for this after all had been no more than one of those ordained moments of low comedy like going over a horse's head into shit, or Lucinda fished out of the dustbin. Once every ten years or so the life of the natural clown met with a proper, natural circus act. Now this one, perhaps the best of the lot, was added—hanging on a cliff, suspended in the fog, saved from destruction by my biographer—retrieved, useful, to disremember with burning cheeks at hours of sleeplessness, nature's comic, but Rick the proximate agent, Rick the accessible, Rick the object, Rick the Prick— There, just under where I'd hung in fog, a meadow stretching away, with cows in it. Tinkle, clonk.

I found I was standing up and trembling with my fists clenched. I turned away and began to walk carefully towards the hotel—carefully because I did not want anything nasty to happen to my old heart at this altitude, I needed to live until Rick got there and I had to do breathing exercises to get some control back, half-blind with fury as I was. My ears were singing and my heart beating somewhere up by the base of my throat. I don't remember the path back or opening doors. I remember looking at the bottle of Dôle and deciding to leave it alone. I told the new fat young woman, who would serve behind the bar for a generation or two then die, that I was going to acclimate, yeah, that was how I said it, the interview with Rick was going to be done at strength ten. I told her that bit. I don't think she understood anything. I hung a "do not disturb" notice on the door, took about a handful of pills and knocked myself out, if anything a little too far, and slept from Thursday afternoon until midday Friday. Then I woke. And after a light lunch consisting of the Dôle I thought I could probably risk, I tried myself out on the path again and really I had acclimated a bit for I reached the stone in little or no time and sat there, feeding my rage like you might poke bits of wood into a fire. I don't know how long that took. Then I kind of tamped it down and went back to the hotel. I walked backwards and forwards in my sitting-room, waiting for Rick to come. I'd forgotten that Friday wasn't Saturday and I had to consult my journal to make sure, but the journal itself seemed confused so I had some more pills and knocked myself out again.

Saturday morning wasn't so good. No, let us have less of this British reticence. Saturday morning was bloody awful. I was so strung up with the wire I thought anyone else in the place—there were three other people staying there but I was able to ignore them—would be able to hear me coming. I remember though, asking the nephew of the manager—well, he *was* the manager—to let me use his typewriter, as you can't buy them in the Weisswald. I typed a carefully considered document. I put this in the middle of my polished table. It lay on the polish very

136

pleasantly and watching it really made the time pass so I sat there, my back to the french windows, my sunglasses hiding the top of my face and I took an occasional swig from the new bottle of Dôle but not too much, as I needed a degree of sobriety.

The knock on the door came some time in the afternoon. It was not a firm knock. I had deliberately left the door on the latch because I did not wish to be seen to do him a courtesy.

"'Come in.'"

Yes, it was Rick, not remembered but there at the time. He came in cautiously, head right up by the top of the door, body still as big but somehow different in shape. Perhaps his chest had slipped a fraction. He stood just inside the door, blinking against the light. Then he looked round the room very carefully as if he suspected an ambush. He peered across the table at me.

"It really is you, Wilf?"

"Yeah."

His mouth widened, showing a lot of American teeth.

"I trust you've had time to acclimatize, Wilfred—sir?"

"Yeah."

He saw the paper. My goodness me, his eyes widened almost as much as his mouth. You could have thought he had no eyelids except—ah, the storyteller's power of observation!—the eyelashes stuck out all round them. A handsome hunk, our Rick.

"In fact, Wilf, I can see your signature!"

"Yeah."

His eyes, unable to widen any further, bulged a bit. I nodded at him.

"Take a good look, son. We'll butt heads. I'm not going to avoid you, like in Navona."

His eyes went back in. I could see that he deepened the corrugations in what was visible of his forehead. Have I told you about his hair? No. Well, Professor R. L. Tucker had abandoned the half-length and gone afro. I mean it. His hair was frizzed and much lighter than erstwhile; and

137

now I saw other things that only a trained observer would notice like for example the clothes he was wearing. His white trousers were flared at the bottom and the gores were sequinned. I'd been so enjoying his eyes that I had neglected all else and now I saw that his shirt, or vest as we say roundabout thirty west, had a huge chunk carved out of it clear down to where his navel would have been in view if that thatch, coppice, undergrowth of Tuckerish hair hadn't hidden it. Well, if you have hair on your chest, why not say so? As it were. But somehow the high fashion of his gear put me right back to being British from the mid-Atlantic ridge I'd been affecting.

"Won't you sit down, professor?"

He sank into the chair opposite and I heard it creak.

"How was Rome, professor?"

"You were calling me Rick, Wilf, sir. When would that be?"

"Come now! Right after I left here last time about a century ago, when you followed me down to Rome. That was clever. Luck too, of course."

But Rick wasn't listening. He had returned to staring at the paper on the polished table as if it might fly away at any moment. To make the situation plainer I took it up and held it.

"There is absolutely no reason for you to do that, Wilf, sir. I assure you."

"How come you speak the way you do, Rick? Years and years in England I don't doubt."

"How come you speak the way you do, Wilf? The tones, I mean. They've flattened."

"Let's not bother about geography, Rick. Just tell me as a matter of interest what you were doing that time in Evora."

His eyes blinked. They were a little less bulging.

"Where's Evora, Wilf?"

"Be your age, Rick. I just wanted to know what you were doing there. Well, I see you're determined to keep your own counsel and after all why not? For the present you'll be interested to hear that I've acclimated. I've been *twice* back to that place. You knew, didn't you? Just down there in the fog with me hanging on for dear life, shit-scared of smashing, perhaps a yard under my feet there was a bloody great meadow, an alp, as they say. If I'd fallen I'd have gone a yard, and then if I'd wanted to fall any more I'd have had to canter across the meadow and throw myself off the other end of it. Don't shake your head like that. You knew. You were up there only the day before spying out the land and you led me back to that place—oh I admit you probably didn't arrange the rock fall but it was all a huge slice of luck for you, wasn't it, the fog, the rock, the rock breaking the rail and me going to lean over? You're a quick thinker, professor, I give you that, you did fool me, you bastard, Rick—"

"No sir, I did not, not in any way—"

"Quote, it seems I owe you my life, unquote."

"But sir, you said that, not I, and—"

"Of course the old insect lent a hand laying his eggs under my carapace, I've no doubt about that, but by Christ you were on the side of creation, weren't you?"

"I don't—"

"If I hadn't had the common cowardy sense to cut and run, God knows what would have happened."

"Wilf, I must tell you. Remember, I'd been all the way out to just under the Hochalpenblick. I only did that once in daylight. With you, it was in fog. I *couldn't* have known the path yard by yard and be sure what was under the fog, gee, I'd have to be a computer."

"You knew."

"OK. So I knew. But what I knew was a guess and I couldn't be sure. Believe me, I thought I was risking my neck there, Wilf, and for you. I swear it."

"Scout's honour."

"You're distressing me, Wilf."

"Have a good cry then. When you've done we'll get on with the dog."

It's strange; but my memory is that Rick's eyes really

139

were filled with water and as if to make the point he took a tissue out of somewhere and wiped them with it.

"After all these years, Wilf—"

"Shut up, man. Don't you want the paper?"

He took a bit of time over that, sniffing and wiping his eyes. When he spoke his voice was smaller.

"Yes, Wilf. I do."

"Righty-ho. Bang on. Good show, Tucker."

"You were calling me—"

"I know, Tucker. Now. Tell me about Halliday. Don't skimp. You can't frighten me, you see. I want every fascinating detail."

It took Rick quite a while to get himself together that time.

"He's a wonderful—well, those who know him—"

"Mary Lou."

"You know she majored in flower arranging and bibliography, sir, so there's a great deal of scope for her in his collection."

"He collected Mary Lou."

"No sir. It's his manuscripts."

"Ha et cetera."

"I know you aren't interested in literary history, Wilf, after all, you're part of it—"

"I'm not interested in history, period. It should be rolled up like a scroll. Halliday! I want more Halliday!"

"For example he'd pay anything for that."

He reached out his hand towards the document I'd typed. I smacked it hard and moved my hand farther away.

"Naughty!"

"But, Wilf—"

"And while we're about it, why are you dressed up like something out of a circus?"

Rick looked down at himself, pondering the little he could see of his own clothes beyond the thicket. Mary Lou had wept into that thicket—or had she? Was that a fact or an imagination? I found to my surprise

140

that I couldn't distinguish between the two.

"What's wrong with the way I'm dressed? Hell, I was wearing this and more the last time you saw me. Then I had my necklace on. I've put it away because I didn't think the Weisswald was the place for it."

"Don't be wet."

"Well. It isn't."

"I don't mean that. The last time I saw you, you were as trad as the Beatles. Come on, Rick. I know all about it."

"And you come on too, sir. You waved that paper at me!"

"When? Where?"

"Marrakesh. Remember?"

"Rick—"

"I must say it wasn't very kind of you, Wilf. But then I've always allowed that you and the few people like you have privilege."

I examined his eyes carefully. They were like a politician's after he's had more exposure than he can take, more anxiety, belief, accommodation, ambition, suspense. There was white showing all round the irises. It's not an infallible mark but it does reveal a degree of strain, tending towards what I said about hell. It can indicate pain too, or fear. Well, why not? Man bites dog.

"Tell me about Marrakesh then, Rick."

"Must I? Oh well. It was outside the Hôtel de France. For God's sake, Wilf! It'll be in your journal somewhere, you've only got to look!"

"More. Come on. More details!"

Rick flung his arms wide. It was so unlike him I knew how desperate he was.

"You were on the balcony to the left side of the main door—first floor. You saw me. You laughed and waved the paper at me. Then you disappeared into the building— what a joke for you! I can take a joke, Wilf."

"How did you know the paper was permission to be my literary executor?"

"What else could it be? I didn't mind the joke, Wilf,

only—like I said I went in to reception but they said you weren't staying there. I said to myself you were visiting with someone and I went up to the first floor and knocked on doors and listened."

"You must have been popular."

"You could have helped. A joke is a joke like I say, but when they threw me out—an American, Wilf. That hurt."

"Rick."

"Huh?"

"When was this?"

He thought, frowning.

"Six—no, seven months ago."

"The last time I saw you, Rick, was just over a year ago. You were walking down one side of the cloisters in that hotel in Evora. You were wearing a light grey suit and you were walking away so you didn't see me. I had to leave at once."

"I have never—"

"Quiet. If I say I am going to tell you the exact truth and swear by all that I believe in, heat, light and sound, intolerance, necessity—would you believe me?"

"Yes sir. Yes I would!"

"Rick. I say this with all the force and all the precision at my command. I have never been to Marrakesh!"

Pause.

His eyes popped! I mean by that, the white round the irises widened then as suddenly seemed to narrow. He let out a long breath and laid his two hands flat on the table. Deliberately he made of his eyes the normal ellipse or near-ellipse with the irises partly covered. He seemed not so much to deflate as to come down to his true size from some sustained effort to make himself imposing. He began to smile. He nodded and nodded.

"Of course. I see it all, Wilf. It was somebody else. I'd been thinking so much about you and the need for me to do your biography and Mr Halliday always on wanting it, and then after picking up clues here and there, to see someone just like you—"

"The hunter and the slain."

"—and, hell, you got a beard, Wilf, and all those Ayrabs got beards—"

I was nodding in time to his nodding. Two porcelain mandarins. I smiled at him helpfully.

"I expect you were looking into the sun."

"Why that coulda been it, Wilf. Yeah. South-west at that time, just after siesta, the sun right above the hotel, above—that man I saw laughing and waving a paper at me—"

"You see? Simple."

"But right now I know where you are—"

"You don't know where I am. Nobody knows."

"Why surely, sir, there's no need—but now we can keep in touch, and you, being what you are—"

"You don't know who I am! Nobody knows who I am!"

"No, no. Of course not. OK, sir. Look we'd better—"

"Halliday now. He knows. No one else."

"We'd better—"

"Say 'Yap yap'."

"I don't get it. Are we playing a game?"

"That's right, professor. Say 'Yap yap'."

"Yap yap."

I let out my breath and sat back. I unfolded the document and read it through. It seemed solid enough but then I was struck by the thought that of course it should have been vetted by a solicitor. I was vexed to think of having wasted so much time and effort; but after all there were solicitors or lawyers in Zurich. I was a little cross with myself, however, and brooded.

"What do you say now it's your turn, Wilf?"

"Turn?"

"This game. You know. 'Yap yap'."

"Oh that! I don't say anything."

"I don't get it, Wilf."

"All will be revealed in time."

"That paper, Wilf—"

"You don't get that either. Now don't take on so, Rick

143

old friend. My chum the manager's nephew and the new young fat woman will throw you out. I mean you don't get this one. But if you're a good, shall we call it, fellow, you'll get a nice piece of paper signed and sealed—"

"Wilf, sir, I don't know how to—"

"—when to and where to. However. There are necessary preliminaries."

"Anything! I got less than two years left, Wilf. You just don't know—"

"That bad?"

"Anything. Yes, sir."

"Well, as we agreed, I have to know the whole set-up between you and you-know-who."

"Mr Halliday?"

I bowed my head solemnly. Rick scratched his nose and looked puzzled. He was at ease though. Happy.

"It's simple enough. He staked me, you see. Seven years so I could devote myself to—"

"How long does he get Mary Lou for?"

"Mary Lou has ceased to mean anything to me, sir."

"You don't even get the occasional use?"

There was a long pause. I broke it, helpfully.

"A hard taskmaster, Mr Halliday. If you haven't brought me to heel in seven years and achieved my authorized biography—incomplete, of course, as I am still to some extent on stream—there'll be wailing and gnashing of all those lovely teeth."

"He ceases to support the research. But listen, sir. I'm not helpless. I can go other places—"

"Don't be wet. There is but one of them. I thought at first, oh years and years ago, I thought it was like you might say Guggenheim or Fulbright but not so. She wouldn't have gone just for the money, Rick, and I wouldn't be all screwed up, strung up and you strung up. You see? It's like trying to serve me and him or it, it's like serving God and Mammon. Guess which is which."

"You promised that paper or one like it! You'll not go back on your word, sir!"

144

"I won't. But you didn't give me time to lay down conditions, did you?"

"I can't remember. This is awful."

"I'm not giving you this paper yet and I'm not giving it to you here. You have to do certain things."

"Anything—"

"I am going to allow you to write the official, the authorized biography of Wilfred Barclay, you lucky, lucky man. I shall give you relevant information. I shall appoint you custodian of all material concerning me."

"I swear—"

"I shall oversee the biography word by word."

"Surely, surely!"

"We shall meet at a time and place decided by me."

Then he deflated all over again.

"But, sir—Wilf—your health—"

"You mean I might, like, drop dead?"

"No, sir, but your memory it isn't all it might be. Writers are absent-minded, you know that, Wilf."

"Not so absent-minded I'd put all my chips on one number the way you did. You see, I hold you in my hot hands. I permit you. Just that. You get a permit. I get a commit. Just that."

"Sir."

"Tomorrow morning I am going away again. I wish never to revisit this place where—I shall get in touch. You are not to follow or the deal's off. At some point or other you can introduce me to Halliday."

"That's real difficult."

"But you, wonderful you, can do it. You have the entrée."

"No, sir, Mr Halliday doesn't give that to anyone without she's real pretty."

"No boyfriends? No bestiality? No real kinky stuff, torture, murder? What's his billions for, just *ewige Weib* or whatever they call it? Well, Rick. You know how we really knowledgeable people are returning to the primitives to regain our health. One of the— My

145

dear, Rick, I feel a lecture coming over me!"

"If you'll only hold on a moment while I get my recorder out—"

He slid the camera from his sleeve.

"That?"

"Sure. It takes pics too. But, Wilf, I have never been near you without this up my sleeve only there sometimes it misses things so it'll be better standing on the table."

"You've never recorded me!"

"Yes, sir, always, even at dinner way back in your house. My one regret is I never got that time in the night when we met."

"I don't believe it!"

"And I got you even earlier than that, sir. Not on this machine of course but way back when I was a student. Why I swear in between even your accent's changed!"

"Don't be wetter than you need be. My accent is satellite and always has been."

"No, sir."

"Earlier? Back before you were with me and Liz?"

"When you were in the States. I'll play it back to you one day."

"No you won't. On footsteps of our dead selves or something. You'll wipe the lot or the deal's off again."

"They aren't mine sir."

There was a long pause after that as I digested it. Of course. Halliday had them in the Barclay foundation. They as well as Mary Lou were part of the deal. The lord giveth and the lord taketh away, cursed be the name of him whatever one he chooses. Who knows his place? Who can affront, outface, attack, overthrow him? We can do nothing but strike his ministers in the forehead with a stone and hope it sinks in.

"Wilf, you were going to say a piece."

"Ah yes. This lecture. It's about rites of passage. *You* know about them, Rick, I'm talking to myself. For example a rite of passage is when you find that instead of fishing round for tintacks—thumb tacks you'd call them—in some

146

saucer of mum's, ashtray, paten, rich trifle on the mantelpiece or overmantel as toffs say you can walk into a shop and buy a whole packet. Then you know what you've done. You've become a householder. Another one comes when you kill something deliberately, a dog perhaps. Reminds me, what do you drink?"

"Anything, I guess."

"Bourbon? They tell me bourbon's come back in. Vodka? Whisky? I stick to wine myself."

"I'd like that, Wilf."

"When you have a vision of the universal wrath, intolerance—well hell, Rick, it isn't a vision the way they get painted here and there, say in Italy, it's real like a rock and you know it's for ever like diamonds. That's a rite of passage."

"Yes, Wilf."

"You recording?"

"I guess so."

"Clever little thing! I feel like some coffee. Could you go and get me some coffee, Rick? Just to show the machine how much you venerate the old man?"

He rushed off with the kind of eagerness a child might show when after being rebuked he is assured that the sun has come out again. I sat and stared at the machine. I made funny noises at it since the camera function wasn't taking any notice of faces. Rick came back with a small tray and coffee for two.

"We'll have some wine first, Rick old friend."

"Whatever you say, Wilf."

"Just fill one of the saucers with wine, Rick."

"Sir?"

"Well, whatever did you think I needed coffee for? To drink? Of course, come to think of it, tea would have done just as well."

Rick put the tray down on the table. His eyes were bulging again. He sank into the chair across the table from me.

"This is a rite, son. After a rite nothing is ever the same

147

again. You can go to bed and get up again and go on doing that till hell's blue and nothing changes. This is different, isn't it? Let's see where we are? You will get authorization, like I said. But what assurance have I that you will keep your side of the bargain? So you'll do anything. Just to prove it—just a friendly test, Rick. Take one of the saucers and put some Dôle in it."

I waited, interested. He did nothing.

"Come, lad. You've been following me and recording me and pestering me and, yes, tempting me and persecuting me and buying and selling me all for the purpose of your lout literature. Are you going to fail now? Why—think of the chapter on Wilf's accent!"

He was breathing hard.

"Yeah."

"What do you mean, 'yeah'?"

"Your Limey accent."

"Too, too crude, Rick. Like I said, I'm satellite."

"No, sir, I don't mean now, I mean way back."

"A fat lot you know about it!"

"I got an ear. Had an ear. That was why I did phonetics. I was real good. I *am* real good. But there's no future— Well. My prof said to get a sample of you for the archive. I was working my way through college and I couldn't be there. A friend of mind did the job. He got it fixed up, a recorder under the guest chair in the Faculty Club. Later on I couldn't believe in you when I heard you. Those diphthongs! And the tones—my God they were near enough Chinese."

"I was listened to in complete silence and with great respect!"

"No, sir. Not what you said but the way you said it. Then later—*what* you said."

He was standing up, gripping the edge of the table and leaning forward.

"They made a kinda party piece out of that record, Wilf. When I got my dee fill they played it at the party. No, sir, it was not my doing so don't blame me. I'm just telling you,

148

sir. In fact that party was the first time I listened to what you were saying, 'stead of picking out phonemes. I was real sick of phonemes by then.''

I found I had been standing too. I sat down, heavily.

"That's vicious. That's really vicious!''

"No, sir. Apart from the sounds it wouldn't have been funny except for the coincidence. You were going on about the British social system—said the British were Greeks and the Americans Romans. You went on about the 'Spartan incorruptibility' of the civil service. You gave examples of their perfect devotion, like traditionally conservative civil servants organizing the nationalization of industry for the socialists. Only of course when he played the tape at my party we'd just heard the way your civil service was full of Philby and those guys. Laugh? People were falling about. They were real sore, too. Your civil service hadn't just dropped you in the shit. They'd dropped *us*! You and your Limey accent!''

I found to my surprise that I was gripping my side of the table the way he was gripping his.

"That was most unwise of you, Rick, if you'll forgive my elaborate Limey way of putting things. You let yourself go, didn't you? Now we know, don't we?''

The fire began to die down in him. He was deflating, returning to that state which I now saw not to be vacant, ignorant or servile but inscrutable. We were learning.

"You've shot your bolt, son. Wine in the saucer if you would be so kind.''

He still waited.

Tucker. Tucker the fucker.

"No wine in the saucer, no authorized biography. No letters from MacNeice, Charley Snow, Pamela, oh a whole chest full of goodies! Variant readings. The original MS of *All We Like Sheep* which differs so radically from the published version. Photographs, journals dating right back to Wilf's schooldays, the happiest days of your life, Tucker, when you get your claws into it—a placated Halliday. You will be able to get off

149

your knees. The pearly gates will open. A modest fame."

"Scholarship—"

"Balls."

Heavily he reached out his hand, heavily poured Dôle into one of the little saucers.

"Put it on the floor."

For the first time in my life I saw eyes literally fill with blood. There were blood vessels in the corners and they engorged. I thought for a moment that they might burst. Then he laughed with a kind of crack and I laughed with him. I shouted yap yap at him and he shouted it back and we laughed and he put the saucer down on the floor laughing and he got on his knees having caught on and understood what was required of him. I could hear him lap it up.

"Good dog, Rick, good dog!"

He leapt to his feet and hurled the saucer in my face but I knew Who I was and the saucer passed by my ear. It hit a curtain and fell to the floor. The pile of the carpet was thick enough to receive it gently. The saucer didn't even break but rolled round in diminishing circles then fell over the right way up. Tucker collapsed in the chair. He deflated further than I have ever seen, seeming to come in on every side so that his very clothes hung on him like sails that have lost the wind. He put his face in his hands. Only then could I see that he had begun to shudder like a man in deep shock. A dog. He sat there, leaning forward, face in hands, elbows on the polished table.

I turned my attention back to the intolerance and insolently interrogated it.

How's that?

Water was coming through between his fingers. Sometimes single drops fell straight down on the polish but sometimes they would be included in the sobbing and through a shake they would be flicked out into the air and thus come halfway across to my side. His weeping became noisy. I have never heard a sound from as deep down and as hard to get out, like bone breaking up. It took the will of

150

his body away so that he slumped, his elbows sliding back off the table, hands open on either side, cheek flat.

"Can you hear me in there?"

His hands slid off the table too. I could imagine his arms hanging straight down, knuckles perhaps on the floor, like an ape's.

"I said, 'Can you hear me in there?'"

"I can hear you."

"Right. Let's get round to business."

He heaved himself up so that he was sitting, hunched. He didn't look at me. All the same I could look at him. His face was streaming wet, eyes red, but no longer with engorgement. It was more like smears.

"Must we now? I guess I want to sleep or something."

"Have another drink."

He shuddered.

"No, no!"

I looked at my paper again.

"I shall make you my literary executor, probably in association with my agent and either Liz or Emmy-Emmy, perhaps. I shall authorize you to write my biography while I am still alive but with reservations I have not yet detailed."

Rick yawned. He really did!

"Pay attention, son!"

"Sorry."

"After I have taken legal advice on the proper form of the document you will sign, I shall communicate with you again, appointing a place for us to meet. Is that all clear?"

He nodded.

"Well, there we are then. Remember me to Helen if and when you see her again. Give Halliday my best wishes as from one banker to another. I imagine he has a bank."

"Quite a few."

"Tell him to keep up the good work. A wit, your Mr Halliday. Or have I said that before?"

"Yes sir."

"Total recall, Rick. Well. I imagine that's all. Unless of course, you have any queries?"

"Yes, sir—Wilf. How long do you estimate? Time is—"

"Precious. Not mine, it isn't. However, in your case I suppose— Well. It might be a week or two or a month—or two. Not longer. What difference can it make to you? You have no settled employment, ex-professor."

"And you did say, Wilf, you mentioned reservations."

"Ah yes. They only refer to the biography, you know. Nothing to worry about."

He looked at me, miserably and warily.

"I'd like to know, Wilf, if it's all the same to you."

"That's reasonable, Rick, and I thought that perhaps you would want to know them before you committed yourself. I'll mention the principal one so that you can think it over. I shall give you a full and free account of my life without concealment and you can write what you like about that. But you will also give a clear account of the time you offered me Mary Lou and of the time you offered Halliday Mary Lou and had the offer accepted. In fact the biography will be a duet, Rick. We'll show the world what we are—paper men, you can call us. How about that for a title? Think Rick—all the people who get lice like you in their hair, all the people spied on, followed, lied about, all the people offered up to the great public—we'll be revenged, Rick, I'll be revenged on the whole lot of them, ha et cetera. In this very room, my son—Mary Lou and me and you off to sleep, seduce the old sod, 'Rick Tucker, who I am sure will entertain you', did you forge that too, from the old poet whose boots you probably licked just to say you knew him? It's a trade, my son. Me for you. My life for yours. Don't say you won't do it. You have to do it there's nothing else you can do you have to lick the platter clean like the saucer down there the flying saucer Christ you can't even throw straight. Now you know. Sod off and come when I call you. I'll whistle."

So we were silent again. I had time to reflect that a really *manly* man of Rick's size would pick me up and chuck me over the balcony down to smash. But Rick was a paper man. There was no strength in him. I was safe, had been deceived. He wasn't strong or hot or warm. He wasn't a murderer. He was a suicide if anything but I doubted even that. Suicide is a sickness in health and Rick was wholly sane. It was his one—no, he *had* a crack. Marrakesh.

But the man was standing up. He was inflating I saw. Was he going to be what Johnny would call "cruel" and do me a mischief? I found to my surprise that I did not care. I watched him, eye to eye, perhaps for the last time I thought. I held him with the power of the human eye over a beast. So at last he looked down and turned to the door. Then when he had reached it instead of going straight out as I had thought he would, he turned suddenly, swelled. He clenched his fists and yelled at me.

"You mother-fucking bastard!"

Then he was gone.

Well, well, I thought! There are moments when one's pets surprise one. Sometimes they are almost human. You'd swear they know what you're talking about. Dear Fido! Of course they never bite. They merely growl in fun and seize master's hand with hurtless jaws. Besides, it's company.

I sat back and looked round the sitting-room in which we had held our kind of joust with paper lances, or at most old-fashioned biros. The saucer still lay on the carpet. I let it lie with a feeling that it had ceased to be just a saucer. It was now like all those objects which have received *mana*, power. Probably it *was* a flying saucer, visiting. What the hell. Then again what about the drops of water on the table? Some of them were smeared I saw and the rest drying with a tiny line of whatever salts they contained already showing round each. Probably in magic there was great virtue in such drops. Virgin tears? If you can find the tears of a grown man, my son, gather them up at the full moon and they are a sovran remedy against boredom, flatulence, world-weariness: and are one in the eye for old intolerance who thereby is getting its own back.

I poured myself some Dôle. I looked at it and somehow seemed not to want to drink it which was absurd. The moment he had disappeared I had become more aware of the steel string and now it seemed to be not merely tight but cutting into my chest. I forgot Rick and concentrated on the string which by magic now ceased to be length with little breadth but widened into a band, then into a strap. I felt as if it were tightening all over me, even my head, my head. Then I was shuddering and yelling and fingering my flies like a kid in a kindergarten.

Chapter XIII

This bit can't be connected. I cannot, simply cannot remember the succession of events that followed our second meeting in the Weisswald. The wire came in too close, was too tight. I have to remember in scenes as if I had reels of film with great gaps. One scene is in Zurich where I found a lawyer though I can't remember how. He was a she and when she found what the agreement contained she looked at me more as if she was going to buy me rather than do me a service. She was small and wrinkled and one of those women who combine an extreme ugliness with an extraordinary degree of femininity. I don't mean a *jolie laide*. That phrase puts the subject straight into the sexual mess where we are not, nor were not. She had a kind of security—that kind which stems perhaps from getting on very well without some of our less attractive qualities, such as the need for revenge, more success than other people, protection from other people or indifference to them. I remember thinking it was a good job I was no longer bothering with writing beautifully a Wilfred Barclay book because she again was a real person and useless to the novelist because he cannot describe them and they do not bother to describe themselves, existing more in their silences than their speech. I am still not clear how she got me to see that I didn't need the document at all but could leave the business for the time being as I had no intention of meeting Rick again until the steel wire was slackened a bit. I remember ending our time together envying her bitterly. The things you could see that woman had no need of!

The other thing, other reel I have from Zurich was about

a graveyard. The thing is that the stone had the man's date of birth on it and nothing else. Later I remembered the date and it was my own date of birth. There's no doubt about it. I sat in one of those plastic hotels you get in big cities and saw the stone with my mind's eye and read the date letter by letter. There was room left for the rest. So I got back on the road again with a hire car. I must have gone high to get across the mountains and this was—I think—because a hearse kept following me. I must have dodged it by going up a side road, one of those that are only used by foresters. There are blank bits here because I remember coming down the Italian side and finding the treeline below me. God knows where I'd been. Then I stopped because I'd detected a movement in the earth. Well, where I was, it wasn't earth but mud. The track was stones and gravel with nasty drops round it here and there and outcrops of rock which hadn't done the hire car any good. Well, I sat in the driving seat, and I saw old roots and bits of tree trunk or branches sticking out of the mud beyond and above me and the thing is they were moving. Then I saw that all the mud was moving down, the skin tearing and mending itself and the sticks and things writhing as in pain or waving as if for help of which there was none, natch. It hadn't occurred to me you could have an avalanche of mud but there it was and it missed my hire car but cut the track so that not even a tank could have got through. I had to slither and slide and climb and scramble. I came on Italian workmen doing things to the road at the bottom and when I explained I'd left my auto up at the top they laughed at me. I had a lot of being laughed at and fuss.

I have a reel about being back in the colossal motel and having the same dream over and over again. I must have stayed there for weeks, it was so impersonal. The place I mean. It stuck up, concrete sticking out of a concrete wasteland. This dream was I'd be in Marrakesh where I'd never been and I'd be running away from Rick who was chasing me in a hearse. My only course was to run out into the Sahara beyond roads so he couldn't catch me. I'd

156

spend the rest of the dream out there. Dream by dream the beginning got left out, shortened, or implied until I was having a dream just of being out in the desert. It was everywhere and it was just the essence of experiencing unpleasantness. I suppose I was always naked for I don't remember (re-visualize) clothes. There was compulsion. It wasn't the usual, indescribable, rootless, pointless compulsion of dreams and nightmares. It was logical because it followed on the fact. You'll know those pathways of duck-boarding they put across beaches in hot climates so you can get to the sea without roasting the soles of your feet? Well, here there wasn't any pathway, just the sand which was very hot, oh very hot, oven-hot. There wasn't any sky that I was aware of over this desert or if there was my attention was fully occupied with the sand. You see the logic of the compulsion? Christ, how I had to move, dance, run, jump up and down! It was better in the air if that's what lay above the sand so getting one foot out was the best I could do since even in dreams I'm no dab hand at suspending the laws of gravity. However, using all my mighty dream-intelligence, I evolved a compromise that given time might even be a solution to the problem. I bent down and endured my burning feet while with my hand I made a hole in the sand. It seemed logical at the time that this should result in a hole so deep and black it was sickening, like a hole in the universe, but it wasn't burning sand. If I bored enough holes I had a space to put a foot and escape the burning; at which point I would wake up. Sometimes when I stirred the sand with my hands I found I was writing a strange language or making pictures and this would give me room for both feet and I would wake up. But my real trouble began when I took enough pills to knock me out flat because it meant I didn't dream which was of course the object of the exercise but the dreams simply waited for me and when I woke up there they were, and I would have them in the bar or wandering round the concrete waste in which, no matter how hard I tried, I couldn't make a hole with my hands and all I did was call attention to myself. I must have moved on. However, the dreams came too.

There's telepathy. There must be, otherwise there was no reason at all why my other reel should be of where it was, that's where Liz and I had a honeymoon the year before we got married.

I'd avoided it since the divorce. I'm not a sentimentalist and if I were, what the hell would I be doing going back to a place where that all began? But somehow I got there. They knew me after a bit, the hotel filing system being what it is, and by some extraordinary means someone had stuck my gold credit card in my passport which apart from another hire car was all I brought with me. So there I was in the hotel and I went across to the sleazy one and got them to send my sacks of mail across. I walked both ways.

I'd forgotten to say this reel is about Rome, no, not religious Rome but hotel Rome. You get to Piazza what's-it with the fountain in the little boat and then up the Steps and the hotel is at the top. There's a church up there too but the glass is lousy and the hotel far, far preferable. It's a very understanding hotel. They turned my hire car in and gave me the room I wanted, one with a balcony because if you have things you don't want to think about you can always look at the view and fashionably dislike the Victor Emmanuel monument though it's better than most of the rest of the crummy Roman architecture, you can see I have no taste. In any case my desert kept getting in the way of the view. Now here is a remarkable thing and I regard it as being in the same line of phenomenon as Padre Pio and Wilfred Barclay, bank clerk, it's all in the mind. The fact is that even when I was awake and sober my feet were beginning to hurt and so was my hand. That made me change hands in the dream when writing or drawing but I only made both my hands hurt. So I would spend a lot of time in the bathroom with the cold tap on, sitting on the edge of the bath with my feet in the water and putting one hand at a time under the tap. It helped to a certain extent. In fact I must draw your attention to another of those farcical incidents to which Wilf is subject, he had the stigmata like St Francis only in reverse as it were, for being a mother-fucking bastard as my best friend would say instead of getting them as a prize for being good. I make a joke of it as indeed it does not need to be made, being one already but believe me it was no fun. The whole situation was thoroughly out of hand. I remember one evening—no. It's a separate reel.

One evening when my feet and hands were just about bearable and I could see the skyline I was sitting on the balcony trying to get things together. I'd found myself wandering in Rome that morning because I'd been looking for *Who's Who in America* meaning to get a line on Halliday. I'd discovered the Steps again at last. They were littered with dropouts, hippies, junkies, drabs, punks, nancies and lesies and students, as usual, and all of them were wearing guitars or playing them very badly or trying to sell the tin shapes they'd cut out and spread round on the stairs as necklaces or rings or earrings or noserings, there were carpets of artificial flowers and so on. It was a toil getting up but nobody minded me or tried to sell me anything the way they would have if I'd looked as if I could afford to buy. But looking at them I realized what a mess I must be myself and I went up to my balcony and put my head between my hands and tried to think. I decided I'd use my journal to get things straightened out and understand what the score was. Then of course I remembered that I hadn't got my journal; and I had an instant picture (reel) of myself here and there in Switzerland and Italy duly writing my journal in telephone books or on walls or the windows of cars or on lavatory paper then wandering on wherever I might be going if anywhere. I also had a glimpse of myself that very morning, looking in *Who's Who in America*—why had I not seen the dreadful significance? For the page that should have contained Halliday's entry was bare, bare, bare, just blank, white paper! Oh then I started up, feet or no feet, and I was looking across at that same church with the lousy glass and my God he was standing on the top. He was, and I fought my way back into the bedroom from the balcony and sat there on the bed, burning and trembling. I started to shake. I reasoned that I had to stay awake because if I fell asleep he would simply step across from the roof and collect me. Also of course, pills and drink, either or both were out because either or both would render me helpless and unable to resist him if he should choose to step across anyway. This last consideration tightened things altogether. I don't know how long I sat, shaking and staying awake. I know a woman came in to make the bed but I was sitting on it and it wasn't unmade so she went away again; and another man came but from the hotel and not from the next roof so I wasn't afraid of him and ignored him. In the war I had a boil, oh one hell of a boil as a result of my wound, and it swelled and it swelled and there was the time—half an hour it may be—when the pressure from my heart pushed the pus so hard against the skin that it was pain enough to make a man faint. I remember I couldn't believe that the pain would increase but it did. Well the tightening went on, it drew in and in. I suppose I slept or went into some mode of being that wasn't quite being awake or simply being mad.

You could say that I dreamed.

I was standing on the roof next door where Halliday had stood. I was looking down at the steps. There was sunlight everywhere, not the heavy light of Rome but a kind of radiance as if the sun were everywhere. I'd never noticed before, but now I saw, looking down, that the steps had the symmetrical curve of a musical instrument, guitar, cello, violin. But this harmonious shape was now embellished and interrupted everywhere by the people and the flowers and the glitter of the jewels strewn among them on the steps. All the people were young and like flowers. I found that he was standing by me on the roof of his house after all and we went down together and stood among the people with the patterns of jewels and the heaps of flowers all blazing inside and out with the

160

radiance. Then they made music of the steps. They held hands and moved and the movement was music. I saw they were neither male nor female or perhaps they were both and it was of no importance. What mattered was the music they made. Male and female was of no importance for me, he said, taking me by the hand and leading me to one side. There were steps going down, narrow steps to a door with a drum head. We went through. I think that there was a dark, calm sea beyond it, since I have nothing to speak with but with metaphor. Also there were creatures in the sea that sang. For the singing and the song I have no words at all.

I woke up not singing but crying; or of those tears it is better to say that I wept and went on weeping. Believe it or not I was drunker when I woke than when I went to sleep and the tears were flowing so that when I found where I was I examined the bed to see if I'd pissed myself but I hadn't. The bedspread and pillow were wet with tears like in books. Even so the boil had burst, the pain and the strain had gone because I knew where I was going myself, or rather the direction in which I was facing and that there was no more need to run. I could walk and the rest of the journey would simply be provided. A woman knocked on the door and brought in croissants and coffee and a bottle of wine. When she came in I was laughing which startled her but I couldn't explain what I was laughing at. She wouldn't have believed it. But the fact is my feet and my hands were not hurting unbearably. They were still hurting but as if a doctor had put some sort of salve on them that hurt because it would heal. I don't think there's a scientific explanation though if you're a scientist you may cook one up and if you've kept up your religion you may cook one up but hell I'm not dealing with fatuous abstractions like religion or science I'm dealing with life I tell you and asisness, *Istigkeit* I think they sometimes call it, how it is to be human though a, quote, mere fish but a

161

queer fish, unquote. It was also because my feet and hands were hurting sort of like funny bones, as if I'd knocked four elbows.

I spent that day in dressing-gown and pyjamas both of which I sent out for, having discovered that my luggage consisted of nothing at all. I spent the next few days in the hotel getting tailors and suchlike along to fit me out. I also began to deal with the mail bags and the first letter I opened was from Liz. I précis it here. It amounted to, Capstone Bowers has scarpered. I am past it now & I guess you are. Why not return? The moment I had read that I sent off a telegram saying, yes but few days am rekitting! I would sit on the edge of my bath with my feet under water and my hands under the cold tap while a tailor, it may be, would sit on the loo and we would talk about life or allied subjects. The fact is it took me days and days to come to terms with being happy! You have to acquire the knack or it knocks you clean off your feet. So I talked to tailors and shoe-makers and shirt-makers and hatters and jewellers a most agreeable set of men. I ordered a book for keeping a journal but when I tried to fill it with that same lucid prose which people will find in most of my books, my writing hand hurt like the devil and I had to stop. It was then I began to see things coming together. I saw that intolerance hadn't done with me and there was still a book that I or someone had to write, not a journal but more hippity-hop. As the hypnotist said all those years ago I am a perfect subject for suggestion. I saw how suggestion had altered my books especially *Birds of Prey* and *Horses at the Spring*. I cried a lot and was ashamed of it not being overly accustomed to the lachrymose life. I drank of course as I thought an instant renunciation of the bottle would be dangerous but I *did* ration myself to a daily bottle more or less.

The time came when I began to consider my dog. It wouldn't be a good thing to have him down to the house before I'd discovered how he stood with Liz and Emmy. I thought I'd make an appointment with him at the sleazier of my clubs, the Random. I thought I'd talk Rick over with Liz. I envisaged us sitting either side of the kitchen table where we'd had such good times and rows.

That was a strange time in the hotel! There I would be on the balcony, facing the dung-coloured city half as old as time and trying to understand why my dream had been more than a dream and more than being awake. Then I'd consider the book I had to write, picking a story out of a mess. I'd consider its recipient and think how my feet and hands would stop hurting when I finished writing. Then I'd be back in the bath with a bottle on the tray. It may be there'd be a bootmaker sitting on the loo glass in hand and telling me quite fascinating things about his clients and I'd stow the information away in my mental filing system, quite forgetting I had no use for it. Always my mind would come back and dwell in the dream. I began to move about a bit and had the dream explained to me in, let me see, yes, scientific, psychiatric, religious, and *isness* terms (that last from the shirt-maker) all of which are mutually exclusive or so it seemed. Mostly I brooded on the isness. Why this harping on isness? you'll ask. Are you up the wall? you'll say. Isn't quote reality unquote good enough for you? Well the answer lies in the genius of the language. This wasn't reality which is a philosophical concept but quote isness unquote a word from the seamy side of speech for the involuntary act of awareness. I've invented it myself because the dream didn't happen to a philosopher but to me. Religious, scientific, psychiatric, philosophical, all straight up the spout!

Eh violà! Non, voici.

Chapter XIV

At last I was kitted out but still I didn't climb on a plane. It wasn't a lack of mobility. I was able to move, though like an old man. I mean really old, not just in the upper end of the sixties. It was fear. I wanted to go quote home unquote—oh how I wanted! But I was afraid of England and the spring. I could imagine myself crying like a girl which would be a bore. It was weakness and I reckoned the best thing would be to get rid of my mail which would take me some days. But when I'd read a letter or two it all seemed too much. So I supervised the destruction of the rest in the hotel incinerator and felt much lighter. Whenever I asked any of the staff if they thought it would be helpful now to lay off the booze altogether they always said yes it would be helpful. I don't know if they knew what they meant by helpful, just be a good thing I suppose. But then, if put to it, everyone thinks that giving up drinking alcohol would be a good thing except people who can't give it up and have to make excuses. In my case I can give it up when I like though it tends to come back at irregular intervals, temporary setbacks as it were in the grand plan of giving up for good. It *is* a good plan and I've stuck to it for more than a quarter of a century.

However—*this* time! Yes, I did give up again for good and life became dull. I got sober and happy and being happy proved to be dull after a bit but one mustn't complain of bread-and-butter, but eat it up, expecting cake later. There was so much *time*! It stretched away towards the night and each day got longer because I would lie awake for hours then wake up early. I didn't dream.

There's nothing to say about the trip home. The only

thing to record is that when I landed at Heathrow I was afraid to go straight home and decided to inspect my clubs. I walked into the Athenaeum and straight out again. It reminded me of that place in the island somehow, though of course the Athenaeum has plenty of windows. I went straight from there to the Random which was OK more or less. In the way things work out the first person I walked into was Johnny. He was looking very smart and wearing his toupée. He cried out.

"Wilf! There must have been a light in the window!"

"Ha et cetera. Good God, you've gone all prosperous!"

"What about you? May I?"

He fingered the lapel of my suit.

"Oh, my dear. It's enough to make one swoon. How much?"

"I don't know. Leave off, Johnny. The barmaid's looking."

"Yes, I will have a drink, Wilf. Yes, I know the rule book says we mustn't treat each other. Two camparis, please."

"Lime and ginger ale, please."

"Wilf! Are you all right?"

"Just laying off for a bit. Johnny, what's happened to you? Has that uncle of yours died?"

"Wilf, you'll never believe. I'm a national figure!"

"Don't be wet."

"I am, I am! I'll slap you!"

"What is it this time?"

"*Well.* You remember my friend who works for Auntie?"

"Which one?"

"The one who runs most of it, Rudesby!"

"Ha."

"*Well.* I thought we'd parted for good but he must have passed the word along—"

"Same school."

"It may have helped. *As* I was saying, they tried me for this and that, all rather up-market, you know, and then by sheer *luck* they tried me for a panel game! My dear, I'm a rave! The very moment the GBP was feeling mellow about us willowy old things, there I am, ready and willing—I swear my post is bigger than yours and you'd never believe what I've been offered for a sherry commercial! But that's a tricky one."

"What's the programme called?"

It was the first time I had ever seen Johnny look bashful. He even blushed a bit; but he held my eye and giggled.

"*I Spy.*"

I giggled too and for some time we could do nothing else. The barmaid looked at us speculatively as if wondering how dirty the story had been. At last I pushed him away, wiping my eyes.

"No wonder you look like the dog's dinner. You, Johnny! You used to think saying 'of' instead of 'have' was the sin against the holy ghost!"

"As Wilfred Barclay used to say, the money's good, unquote."

"How was *Burning Sappho*?"

"A disaster."

"No!"

Johnny came close.

"You won't spread this around?"

"Of course not."

"The bitch was remaindered practically *before* publication. Oh, indecent haste to post with such dexterity—"

"Such bad luck."

"Talking of dogs—"

"Were we?"

" 'Dog's dinner!' "

"Ah yes."

"Did you ever find it?"

"Take me with you, Johnny."

"Well, now, what were we talking about the last time we met in that positively palaeolithic hotel?"

"You tell me."

"I said you ought to try liking someone and to start with a dog."

166

"Ah."

"Well—did you actually find one? You see, you've altered. I'm curious. Come on, Wilf!"

"Ah."

"Don't make mysteries and hide behind your beard!"

"Yap yap."

"Wilfred Barclay going walkies with a poodle!"

"Yes. I found one."

Johnny's face came down towards mine, eager, curious. News, news, news!

"And—?"

"I killed it."

Johnny took some of his drink and thought about me. He looked out of the window at the little garden which was sunny with daffodils and some blue flower—violets, sweet violets perhaps. He looked back at me solemnly.

"That's bad. That's very, very,very bad."

Somewhere, someone beat a dinner gong.

"Well," I said, "I'll go up to my bowl. Yap yap."

Johnny said nothing.

I went up, making automatically for what used to be considered my seat. It was still empty, the one at the table under Psyche, where I'd sat with my agent at one time, my publisher at another and once with Capstone Bowers. Psyche was still there, natch. She's our only valuable *objet*, early Victorian white marble on a malachite pillar and really rather good. She ought to be looking down at Cupid, of course, and holding her lamp to see his face but in the circumstances she always seems to me to be peering at the menu or the wine list and trying to make up her mind what will go with which. I thought it would be a good place for my interview with Rick. This time, Psyche seemed to whisper in my ear that a carafe of house claret wouldn't do me any harm and I had a struggle to resist her. However, virtue triumphed.

It was so natural to hire a car I did it almost without thinking. Then I rang the house and got Emmy who sounded the way she used to when I had forgotten her birthday. No, I couldn't speak to Liz. Liz was lying down and oughtn't to be disturbed.

Well, I thought, you don't wait around for an ex-husband to come home without feeling a bit of strain over it. Look at the way I've been shilly-shallying over meeting her again! Be a man, my son!

So down I drove on the new motor road which rendered the landscape or what I could see of it quite unrecognizable. Where I could see beyond the concrete, England seemed to be producing nothing but daffodils, they were everywhere. How happy and apprehensive a dog I was, yap yap, driving through England with my hands touching the wheel as lightly as possible. My feet weren't hurting any more and I thought, well, that's reasonable—I'm going home!

Emmy met me at the door. She looked even stumpier and glummer than I remembered. I kissed her on one impassive cheek and saw she'd been crying.

"Where is she?"

"The long room."

She left me to go in with the air of someone who has no more to do with the affair which she thinks is ill-advised and will not prosper.

The long room is really two rooms knocked into one. Liz was standing at the farther end and in the darkest corner where she must have run when she heard the car. She had her hands up to her face. I moved forward and she spoke sharply.

"No!"

I expostulated.

"I was only going to show you my suit. St John John nearly swooned."

"You're just the way you used to be. Indestructible. It isn't fair."

"Well, damn it. What did you want back? A basket case?"

"Want back. Well. You'd better look."

She dropped her hands and moved forward. She had

168

gone. I mean without the voice and the sharpness I wouldn't have recognized her. There stood before me a skinny old hag. The life had gone out of her famous hair and it hung in nondescript wisps. She had learned to frown so much that even now when she had no need to her forehead was corrugated. Her cheeks were so hollow it looked as if she had brought some of the shadows of the dark corner with her in them. But what was most directly appalling was the orbits of her eyes, dark brown and sunken so that her head was a visible skull with a macabre slash of violent lipstick across it. She lifted a hand again to touch the hollow of her right cheek as if to assure herself of the worst and I saw that even now she painted her nails to match the vivid, scarlet slash.

"For Christ's sake, Wilf, what did you expect? Mary Lou or something?"

"He's kept up with you then."

"I think he's almost the hardest part of it. Taking you so seriously. I had to laugh."

"Yes. Yes. I suppose so."

"Did you know, no, you didn't, he and Humph, they both had a go at Emmy. Humph because he was, is, Humph, and Rick because of you. Christ, I'd never have believed it, never believed life could be like it. I tried to throw Humph out and he'd go no further than the spare room. Knew he was on to a good thing. The room's there if you want it."

"He's really gone?"

"Scarpered. You'd never believed it." She gestured to her body, cupping both hands. "He scarpered when this began to gallop. Left everything and ran, even left his Bisley gun and his big game books. When your turn comes, Wilf, don't ask the doctors to tell you the truth. They do it."

"I didn't know."

"You're not a day older. Boozing, wenching, living it up—"

"Only boozing. And that—"

169

"Oh shut up. Of course you will again. The thing is, I need someone. That's the fact of the matter and I won't penalize Emmy, not any more. You know? Well. You don't."

"Not really."

"Then I had my great idea. I got hold of Thomas and bullied your poste restante out of him. I thought I'll get Wilf home if it's humanly possible. He's no idea of caring for other people but he's too bloody weak to scarper. It's blackmail, you see."

"This is where we left off only backwards. More or less. Worse, perhaps."

"So it is."

Then we were silent again so you could hear the birds in the orchard and far off a whinny from the other end of the paddock. Elizabeth spoke in her natural, social voice, absurdly conventional.

"Won't you sit down?"

"Well. Yes. If I may."

So there we were, our feet on the warm floor, both seated, one each side of the empty grate.

"I'm sorry, Wilf. I didn't mean it to be—I don't know what I meant it to be."

"When you are better again—"

"As you used to say, ha et cetera. Wilfred Barclay, the great consultant."

"There must be something—"

"There's everything you want in the spare room. Use that bathroom. I use the back one, have all my things there. Mrs Wilson'll cook. Or you can go out. All the pubs do reasonable food these days. I can't stand cooking."

"Feed you up."

"I don't eat."

"You should."

"Don't you know anything? Haven't you seen anything?"

"The war—"

"God, the injustice of it! You booze and wench and lie

and cheat and exploit and posture like a— I've put you to bed, lied for you, covered up for you—and I get cancer just as if I'd boozed away every year of my life!"

There was nothing to say. The shadows of the evening had crept right across the room. Facing me was a blur of brown skull with black eye sockets.

"You always were good at silences, weren't you, Wilf?"

"It was more a case of you not giving me a chance to speak."

"That's a good one! It goes for to restore my belief in your rottenness. Well. Soon you'll be able to talk with no one to interrupt. Happy?"

I said nothing, did nothing. As so often, to speak the truth was impossible; for I was happy indeed—had remained happy ever since the dream. Nothing could alter that, not even poor Liz. The truth was shameful and it was too late to learn compassion or find another dog.

There was too much silence. I broke it at last.

"I'm staying, that's all."

"You must've got religion. Visiting the sick. You can't go, can you? What would the biographers say? A dying woman who bore you a child. You have to stick round, Wilf, and see it through. A slice of life. No writer should be without them."

"All right."

"Robert Farquharson of *The Keyhole* knows. So does Rick Tucker."

"Yap yap."

"That's what he kept saying the other day. I thought it must be some new catch word but I'm not *au fait* these days, don't even watch TV."

She scrabbled for a cigarette in the box on the table by her chair and lit it, then went straight into a coughing fit. She threw the cigarette into the grate but immediately she stopped coughing fumbled for another one.

"You still don't smoke, do you, Wilf? Men! Even Humph was scared of this, this—"

"Illness. Sickness."

171

"—this cancer."

"Look, Lizzie, I'll try to explain. This has struck me all of a heap. But I want to help. I'm not used to helping."

"I'll say! Christ! What is it? Have you been Received? Are you under instruction? What you need is reconstruction."

"You've been saving this up. Go right ahead. Get rid of all the vomit. When you've done I'll try to say—"

"—and you'll succeed. That's one thing about you, Wilfred Barclay, when you do break a silence it may not be significant or profound but for sheer glibness—"

"Will you listen or not? Just tell me. If not, I'll shut up."

She coughed a bit then threw the second cigarette into the grate.

"All right."

So I told her or tried to tell her. I went right through it, from waking up drunk but not drunk and knowing at last what it was like to be happy. I tried to explain the immediacy of the dream that had made everything else a kind of mirage. The longer I went on trying to describe the indescribable the sillier it sounded.

"—it turned me round, you see. I'd been screaming and holding on to time as if I could stop the whole process; but the dream turned me round and I knew that the way I was going, towards death, was the way everybody goes, that it was—healthy and right and *consonant*—here, what's the matter?"

I found I was standing over her. I thought she'd had some kind of seizure or attack but then I saw that she was laughing.

"You utter, utter bastard! You clown! You, you—"

"Look, Liz—"

"You talk about happiness, years away from your own death—"

"I don't mean that! I was trying to tell you that *it's all right!*"

The laughter and coughing were mixed up.

"You get some kind of fancy religion—"

172

I was shouting.

"I found I was part of the universe, that's all!"

Her laughter went eldritch.

"You're not *part* of it, you sod! You're the whole bloody lot! Here am I—"

She burst into tears.

That was when our local doctor called. Perhaps she was expecting him, I don't know. Henry was a master of elaborate tact. Me, he greeted—perhaps the word had gone round—as if I had come back from a weekend in London rather than years away. He greeted Liz as though he hadn't heard her rage and didn't notice the wetness in her hollow cheeks. Indeed he—exuded—a kind of cheerfulness as though he knew that in spite of all the evidence that might be brought by the prosecution, in spite of suffering, darkness and death it was just a game and at some point we should all give up pretending in the tragicomedy we had put on and return to permanent, common-sense awareness.

I took my things up to the spare room and examined it. Once upon a time, Rick had slept there by himself, then later with Mary Lou, and now again by himself. Many others had slept there at odd times. It was a cottagey room, the fireplace still in order and a smallish window that looked up the river to Foxy's Island. When the leaves were off the trees or newly budded as now, you could see to the turn where the milldam was. Even if she hadn't told me I'd have known that Capstone Bowers had slept there—either when Liz's sickness became acute or when they started the final series of quarrels. His books stood on the mantelpiece, *Maneaters of the Deccan*, *The Elephant Gun*, *Rifles, Ammunition and Rifle Shooting*, *Bisley, History and Records*. Above them a horizontal shape of unfaded wallpaper showed where he had hung his "Bisley" gun. I leafed through his books, waiting till the doctor had gone. There were some splendid diagrams, one of where to shoot a tiger—behind the shoulder or up the arse, never in the head if you want to mount. Adages. How to follow up a wounded animal. Shooting for the pot. Good God, poor Liz, living for all those years with this monster!

I left my bags and went downstairs. From the fact that I could hear Mrs Wilson clattering in the kitchen I deduced that Henry had gone otherwise she would be on tiptoe and the dishes muffled. I went looking for Liz but couldn't find her. Emmy was in the long room.

"So you've come back to be with mummy. What a fool."

"You're here."

"That's different."

She wandered away towards the kitchen. I stood in the middle of the room as if waiting for my hostess. Well. I was. Anything farther from a reconciliation or even accommodation—where was the big, warm-hearted and final Barclay Book that had floated before me every now and then since the dream? We were about as warm-hearted as scorpions.

Liz came down from her room, calm and dull. She'd been given something.

"Sorry about that. No, not him. Me. Won't you sit down?"

"I have to go away again."

"Yes."

"No, I'll be back again. It's Rick Tucker. I promised—"

"Yes."

"I'll meet him at the Random. He's not getting the papers, not those, anyway."

"He's mad, you know."

"Yes."

"So he won't like it."

"Well."

We were both silent for a while. Liz took out a cigarette, changed her mind, made a gesture towards putting it back in the box, then threw it in the grate with the others.

"It's odd, Wilf."

"Yes. We shouldn't have married. Ought to have been relatives, brother and sister, it's been that sort of thing, lifelong, always connected no matter what."

174

"I didn't mean us. I meant you and him. The other day I was reading a biography. Mrs Hemingway said, 'Aldous got better. Ernest got worse.' When I read that I thought about you. She said nothing of critics and drudges. You know what? You and Rick have destroyed each other."

Chapter XV

I went to London for three days. I'd have made it more only the club now had an even stricter time limit for staying nights. Somehow I couldn't face the Athenaeum among all the bishops and vice-chancellors. Say what you like about the Random, there isn't a bishop in sight. Come to that, nowadays there's hardly ever a writer in sight. The first evening there was no one about I knew so I rang my agent but he'd gone home, of course. He lives in the country and I realized I didn't even know his address— canny fellow! I thought of a girl but couldn't be bothered or was too old or afraid or too sensible. I looked at some of the theatres and realized I just simply didn't care about them or about the films. I stood on the pavement of Piccadilly and watched the human race off for its evening's entertainment and thought to myself that Liz was right. I was destroyed in that I no longer belonged to that race but to the ghosts and memories of men. I had my dream and the solid pavement was insubstantial beside it. The violin string was either slack or snapped. Intolerance had drawn back and, though still there, was about as relevant to me as church furnishings. It was the dream singing which wasn't singing; and since singing starts just where words leave off, where are you? Face to face with the indescribable, inexplicable, the isness, which was where you came in.

I wandered back to the Random and had a drink to pass the time. Sitting was so peaceful (the place was empty except for two strangers talking earnestly to each other at the bar) that I had another and then another and so on. I *did* slip a bit.

Next day I saw my agent at his office and did a lot of nodding. He wanted to know if I had anything coming along and I said yes but I'd sooner not discuss it as discussion can sometimes harden an outline—the usual stuff—and he also nodded and I saw how anxious he was to get rid of me. Wilfred Barclay won't do much more, you know. He's all washed up and living on his rents. He's gone all indifferent. Maybe it's time we thought about a collected edition. I went back to the Random and spent the day in bed, sleeping—actually sleeping, peacefully, like a babe as they say, inaccurate as usual. I got up round about five o'clock and sat in the snakepit, waiting. Presently Jonquil came in and told me that Professor Tucker was outside. I was surprised she hadn't told him to go right in but all was made clear when I went out to the lobby. He was squatting on the floor with his back against the grandfather clock. His front was open to the navel if you could have detected that spot among the curls but a large gold necklace lay among the thickets and every kind of charm hung from it—the cross of Lorraine, the Eye of Osiris, the Ankh, a swastika the right way round, the pentacle and a dozen others I couldn't recognize. As I came into the lobby, Rick put his tongue out and grinned and barked. I was a little worried that he was up the wall for good and all which though it would solve things in the long run would pose some immediate problems. But after his initial bark he got up and dusted the Random off his seat.

"Wilf, sir, you're looking great!"

"Tell me how."

"Just great!"

He laughed excitedly like a kid that's been promised, yes, today we really will go on a picnic. He was so young. He was so young-looking. Forty. Maybe forty-five.

"And you look great, Rick, just great. Come along."

I led the way to the bar and Rick followed, chiming quietly like a very superior carriage clock.

"A drink or two first, Rick, then dinner. You don't mind

eating here? The food is reasonable and the drink first-class."

Rick was gazing round him, making a mental note of all the Eng. Lit. faces on the walls. He identified them one after another with little cries of triumph.

"But you're not there, Wilf!"

"Not dead yet. Give me time."

We took our drinks back to the snakepit.

"The paper, Wilf. The agreement—"

"After dinner, Rick, there's a good chap."

"It's been so long now—can I phone from here?"

"Of course."

"I'm so anxious to telephone the good news to Mr Halliday. He will be delighted. You like my necklace? To it I attribute the recent, how to say, change in my, my fortunes—"

"My dear Rick, you speak like an Englishman! Yes, I do like your necklace. Doesn't it ever get in the soup?"

"It was in my bag when. Wilf, sir, I have to apologize sincerely. I was not myself. It was just anxiety for I do sincerely see my life's work or as one might say my duty to be the careful investigation of—"

"I know, I know. After dinner."

"—and apologize for what I said."

"For calling me a mother-fucking bastard?"

There was a cry of delight from the doorway behind us. Johnny St John John and Gabriel Clayton were coming through it.

"Rick Tucker, you didn't!"

"Why, hullo there."

"Gabriel, Johnny, Rick. Everybody know each other?"

Beside Johnny's lanky figure Gabriel looked short but he wasn't. He was medium-height and broad as befits a sculptor. He was a bit round-shouldered and this, with his lowering head, gave him some resemblance to a bull. He knew this and was not displeased by it. Now he laid his fist on his forehead in what he thought was the salute of one artist to another then turned back to the others.

178

"'Mother-fucking'," he said. "I see it as a group. Bronze. We can have it in the other alcove opposite Psyche. Wilf will pay. Much more distinguished than hanging on the wall among all those dreary belles-lettrists."

"Gabriel, dear, do us a preliminary sketch at once! Wilf will pose."

"He bloody won't."

"I haven't seen you since Portugal, Wilf."

"I never met you in Portugal!"

"He goes on like this, Rick, you know."

"Yes, sir, I do know. It's remarkable."

"I put you to bed, Wilf. You owe me a meal. I will collect tonight."

"Oh God."

"Me too, Wilf, dear. In view of the positively penetrating analyses of your character with which I have favoured you on this shore or that—"

"Johnny St John John will now favour us with an example of his penetration."

"Another group, Gabriel. White marble, for purity."

"Ha et cetera."

"You are utterly penetrable Wilfred. You'd be perfectly happy with my little homilies if instead of calling you Rudesby I'd called you *cher maître*, wouldn't you now? We all have our ambitions such as they are—a K, perhaps, eh, Wilf? No? All passion spent?"

"You're too clever by half."

Gabriel was already coming back from the bar with two open bottles of claret held cleverly by their necks in either hand.

"This is generous of you, Wilf."

"So I see."

"Glasses, Johnny!"

"I go, I go. Swifter than et cetera."

"You are Rick."

"Yes sir."

"Are you wealthy?"

179

"No sir."

"The day of the rich Americans is past, I'm afraid."

"No sir, it isn't, sir!"

"I am looking for a rich American. Arabs don't go in for sculpture except as an investment."

"He's not wealthy, Gabriel. He's a poor white like the rest of us."

"This man thinks he's poor, Rick. He's kept himself, to say nothing of his chums, for a third of a century in booze and travel if nothing else. He's only got to tell them there's something for sale and the presses roll, banks gape, reviewers sharpen their pencils—"

"Knives. For God's sake, leave me alone. This is a business visit. Rick and I have things to discuss after dinner."

"Well, dear, you can't discuss business in the Random because it's against the house rules, as well you know. Seduction is on, drag, drugs, my dears, bottomry, barratry, the occasional gang bang—"

"Don't be an oaf, Johnny."

"—besides, 'after dinner' is hours away. Personally I've never known a time when drink didn't expedite business—if, that is, it's really business and not some euphemistical employment—oh of course, it should be the business that's euphem—"

"Johnny, you're high. Let's dispose of these bottles at once. It's very, very kind of you, Wilf."

I felt tired and said so but it had no effect on them. Rick, I noted, began to do what I had never seen him do before. He was drinking, not as heavily as Gabriel but feverishly. At last we wandered up to dinner, Rick now talking a bit wildly. His speech had reverted to toneless Middle-West or wherever it came from originally. They all three got higher and higher. Some of the talk was good, particularly Gabriel's. I was dull. It was odd to find myself the only sober one of the four! The turning point came when I explained to Rick that if he got any drunker he wouldn't understand what I had to say to him. Well, Rick, with a

touch of the whimpers rather than belligerence, gave us all
to understand that he wasn't interested in explanations.
He just wanted the agreement. I said, to break things
gently and as it were lead him towards the truth before
revealing it, that the agreement had never been more than
a gentleman's agreement which made Johnny laugh and
laugh. I got a bit angry. Gabriel, with his capacity for
stirring things up suggested that he and Johnny should be
witnesses to the signing. Before I had gathered my wits
together, Rick was explaining the whole thing to them,
Mary Lou and all.

So I had to break in brutally.

"There isn't going to be an agreement."

Rick's mouth opened and shut without anything coming
out of it but a dribble of the wine he had been drinking.

"I'm sorry, Rick, but that's how it is."

"You kay-ant—" He took a gulp of wine, shook himself
and reverted to the mid-Atlantic ridge. "You can't not.
You, you promised me there in Weisswald after I'd. Not
even you. You can't.'

"Listen, Rick, old friend—"

"I say you can't. You don't know what it means. I put
down every chip I got. You don't mean it, sir, Wilf. I can
take a joke—"

"I'm not joking."

"I warn you, Wilf Barclay. I'll write it whether— Look,
sir. It means sheer beggary. I gave up everything. Mr St
John John, Mr Clayton, you're witnesses—"

"Tell us more, Rick, after all we're his old chums."

"I gave up my career like I said. I saved his neck—"

"You did not!"

"I did so! There, in the fog—"

"You threw your wife at me, you followed and spied on
me. Don't make me too angry."

"You angry? God Almighty. You know what he made
me do, sir, gentlemen? I never followed you—or if I did,
why not? It's a free country and you had your fun,
jumping into a cab that time, a taxi, and being on the other

181

Rhine boat and to cap it all, jeering at me in Marrakesh. If you go on like this—I'd meant to respect your wishes—"

"Will you listen?"

"I warn you. I'm not helpless!"

"Oh for God's sake!"

"I'll use the material Mrs Barclay gave me. And Miss Barclay!'

"What material?"

"They told me things."

"Oh my dears! A positive dénouement!"

"Listen carefully, Rick. You're a bit drunk and perhaps—anyway, listen. You're not going to write that particular biography. I'm going to write it myself—"

Rick gave a kind of howl. I've never heard anything like it. Perhaps it's how a wolf howls or a coyote or something strange and wild. Things got very confused after that. I mean he also kneeled down or rather flung himself down on his knees.

He also bit my ankle. For a turbulent moment or two I thought that I was about to experience that massive male strength again but then he was more or less in my lap and his hands went to my head. He got them on my right ear and left cheek and I think he was trying for my eyes with any fingers and thumbs he had to spare. Johnny tried to come between us and Gabriel, trying—I deduce—to pull the table away because of all the glass, got involved with two men from another table who rashly intervened. From what I've gathered since a wave of hysteria swept over the roomful of diners and those sober-suited professional men for the most part joined in. Tables went over, there were tears, people fell about, menus, wine lists, bills, order books, bits of manuscript flew up into the air and seemed to float like snow. People were cut by glass but in general we didn't get much hurt. Even when we try, we chaps aren't very good at that sort of thing. Like Mary Lou, if in no other way, we aren't physical. I dare say there was some scratching and the odd bite, but little more. I lost a little of my beard and one ear was glowing, that was all. I didn't even see what had happened to my "guest". I slept very well.

When I got downstairs next morning the club secretary was standing in the hall. He was looking severe as I suppose was natural. He marked me off on the list he had ready in his hand.

"Mr Barclay, I must ask for your account of what happened last night in the dining-room."

"I can't be bothered. Sorry."

"I have to report to the committee."

"If they want me to resign, tell them I'll go quietly."

"I simply don't know yet how much it'll cost to repair our Psyche."

"Very aptly put, colonel, oh very apt."

The colonel's frown deepened.

"Are you admitting responsibility? If so—"

"Oh what the hell. In a way I suppose. Yes."

I went into the coffee room which was empty except for a waitress and Mrs Stoney who was sitting at the receipt of custom and looking like her name. I had nothing but coffee. When I went to pay the bill, Mrs Stoney swelled a bit.

"Well, Mrs Stoney, what did you think of it?"

"It's not my place to comment, sir."

"Oh come. We shan't see each other again for I dare say they'll sling me out. Come now, sound off, Mrs Stoney, what did you think of it?"

"Your change, sir. Thank you, sir."

"Boys will be boys, Mrs Stoney. Goodbye."

So away I went. I had, I thought, a new shadow behind me, another bit of past to avoid. For even I, with all my quiet happiness, felt a bit humiliated by the ineffectual pothouse brawl. In books they make far too much of what can be read in a face—exaggerate wildly. But I did not care to remember Mrs Stoney. There are some expressions that can be read like large print, most prominent among them, contempt and dislike.

Chapter XVI

I wondered if I could bear to go home but the road unwound just as if things were normal. That was ironical as I soon found. I had been thinking of the roughing up poor Liz had given me. After all, in law she had no claim and Emmy was long past her twenty-firster. What really took me "home" was this MS you're reading, the job I had to do, to make some use, it might be, of the mass of boxed-up papers before I finished with them. Even so I braced myself for it.

And then Emmy met me at the door, red-eyed.

"She's gone."

"Who?"

"Mummy."

"Gone where?"

"You—you—she's bloody dead, that's where."

"When?"

"Just now. This morning. Just your luck. You'd skipped."

Large tears trickled into the drawn-down corners of her mouth.

"It's been years and years, Emily."

"Oh God."

I suppose a father would have put an arm round her, better still offered her a shoulder to wet. But I wasn't a father, only a stranger who was repelled by what fell from her eyes and nose. She was trying to say something but got little of it out.

"I—I—can't—"

Her mouth opened and nature performed a yelling cry there before me in the human face and body. Then I did hold out a hand but she didn't see it or didn't want it. She turned and stumbled away, a plain, heavy young woman and she went down to the river where she used to go and hide as a child when the world was too much for her. I went into the hall, put down my single bag and climbed the stairs.

"Our" bedroom door was opened and the window. The curtains moved a little and a faint sweetness came from the bowl of primroses and seemed a token of universal indifference. Blessed be indifference! Henry moved out of a corner, his cheerfulness if anything less subdued than usual, less subdued than his voice, however, which was little more than a whisper.

"She had no pain. The liver, you see."

Lucky, lucky Elizabeth! Of numberless exits to have been awarded that one!

All the appropriate things had been done. The nurse or Henry or both had worked fast and well. Her watch and her mother's ring lay on the occasional table by the bed. She was monumental under the white sheet. Henry moved forward towards the bed. He turned and invited me silently. Thus enslaved by what was evidently one of the rituals of death I moved forward and stood beside him. He drew the sheet down to her breast and held it there.

Elizabeth looked quite astonishingly and unnervingly like herself. Someone had wiped off the scarlet slash of lipstick and her unadorned face was minatory. I found myself wondering why I had braced myself for changes. It was nothing, the fall of a leaf.

Her eyes snapped open and they stared up at me. The whole world swam round me for a moment and was covered in mist.

Henry was tut-tutting. He was bending over her and doing something, a trick of the trade. He drew the sheet up again.

I found my voice.

"Pennies. Drachmas. Obols."

Henry put his hand under my elbow and turned me. We

185

marched away together and downstairs. I went to the appropriate cupboard and got not wine for us but whisky. I offered some to Henry without thinking, but he smiled and shook his head. I took a pull at the whisky which went the wrong way. What with shock and coughing I was nearly sick. Henry patted my back. The resources of science.

Presently I straightened up and he beamed at me.

"Better?"

I examined myself. There wasn't any question of being "better".

"I suppose so. Yes."

Henry smiled delightedly.

"I'll take care of everything, er, Wilf."

"Yes. I suppose so. Thank you, Henry."

"Well. I'll be going, then."

Still beaming he withdrew.

I went into the garden and pushed through the bushes. Emmy was sitting on the stone seat and peering into the woods across the river. I stood behind her.

"Is there anything I can do?"

"I don't know. You've left it a bit late, haven't you? No. I don't think so."

"People will have to be told. Relatives."

"And the vicar. She was C. of E. every now and then."

"Is he the young chap in jeans, a sweater with a hole in it and an eighth of an inch of clerical collar?"

"That's him, Douglas. He's all right. Last week she was sounding off about me in front of some people. Later he murmured to me, 'Suffering doesn't always improve people.' Down to earth."

"Is there anything, I mean, that I can do for you?"

"As you said just now. It's been a long time."

"For me too. So. If it's any comfort there's rather a lot of money coming your way. From her first, then me."

As Rick once said, we laughed a lot, Liz and I. Now he could have included Emmy.

186

Everything went off OK. A crowd of relatives turned up to the funeral but tended to group round Emmy and leave me alone. It wasn't shyness either. Rick came to the service which Emmy insisted on having and to the cremation afterwards. He sat at the back, crying noisily, and rushed away before the ceremony was over. Later, in the house, I was left alone even more pointedly as people scrummed politely for the smoked salmon and Moselle. Only once a man broke free, one of her relatives I suppose, though I don't know. He may have been a chum of Capstone Bowers sent to depute for he had army written all over him, large, stout, red-faced. I was ready for conversation or even the offer of a drink but he glared down at me for a few seconds, opening and closing his mouth like a goldfish. Then he changed his mind and went back into the mob. I thought of my Italian connection and the come-uppance she gave me. This was an English Home Counties come-uppance. It went far towards confirming me in my rediscovered belief that there are better places.

"Home thoughts from abroad, forsooth!" It made me feel angry.

The young man, Douglas, emerged from the mob hastily as if to pour oil and repair some social damage. He had a black silk front and rather more clerical collar showing than usual. He came to me with the sort of ducking earnestness which reminded me of Rick Tucker in the days when he was really diffident. I was still angry.

"Ah—Douglas, isn't it?—how's the Church these days?"

"Struggling, Mr Barclay. In need of help."

"Money, of course."

He shook his head with decision.

"No. Or not—primarily."

"If it's spiritual assistance you need, you've come to the right person."

"Really?"

"You will find this difficult to believe but I suffer with the stigmata. Yes. Four of the five wounds of Christ. Four

187

down and one to go. No. You can't see the wounds, unlike with poor old Padre Pio. But I assure you my hands and feet hurt like hell—or should I say heaven?"

"I don't think—"

"You don't think people like me should claim such distinctions?"

He was looking round in a worried manner as if, I thought, to find a really good shrink to recommend. Perhaps he would give me the name and address of his own.

"Come, vicar. Don't you find it remarkable?"

"You are serious?"

"Otherwise you'll be off again to those publicans and sinners?"

"Oh no. Or rather—you *are* serious?"

"I should be! At times they hurt like hell."

He looked closely into my face.

"You must be very proud of them."

That took me aback. He amplified with a grin of quite unclerical teeth.

"After all. There were three crosses."

I stood there, seeing the room before me as on a screen— the relatives filing away past Emmy, young Douglas now making his goodbye to her, all the shaking of hands and agreeing that people only seemed to meet nowadays at funerals.

But I was left with so much cleared up! Three crosses— the whole spectrum— Not for me the responsibility of goodness, the abject terror of being holy! For me the peace and security of knowing myself a thief! I stood, saying nothing, doing nothing while they all went away. Emmy came and said something to me, I think, but I didn't catch what. Indeed, I must have sat down at some point but I don't remember doing it. Mrs Wilson must have cleared the mess away but I never noticed her. It was a kind of catatonia.

Next day Emmy said she'd sell the house as soon as I had, as she put it, "fucked off". Then she went back to her social work in some middle-class slum or other and I was left to clear my things out of the house. I found I'd left little but the papers that had so annoyed Liz and Capstone Bowers. It occurred to me, I remember, that without pondering the matter I'd probably meant them to annoy. We don't know much about our current selves, do we?

Rick came and begged me and cursed and yapped. I forbade him the house which is a bit of a joke when you come to consider it. But he hung round, sleeping God knows where and spying on me every now and then round corners. Since my dream I've been as certain as your average sane man could be when people are really there and when they aren't. There's no doubt at all, Rick is really there and spying on me. He hasn't the least idea that I have it in my power and what is more in my purpose to heal him. I'll get him his dream. Wilfred Barclay the great consultant.

Capstone Bowers rang. He didn't come to the funeral but had the cheek to demand his books and his gun. I hung up on him. I ought to add he'd drunk what used to be my really brilliant cellar and not kept it up.

I've spent the time, since Emmy went, in ploughing through some of the piles of paper from the tea chests; but mostly in typing and brooding on this brief account. Yesterday I reread at a sitting the whole thing from Rick at the dustbin down to Douglas at the funeral. The wake. Ha et cetera.

Putting aside repetitions, verbals, slang, omissions, it's a fair record of the various times the clown's trousers fell down. At my age there can't be many more. I do think the best of the lot, the real, theologically witty bit of his clowning, was surely the stigmata awarded for cowardice in the face of the enemy! But St Francis and all the other suggestible creatures didn't just get it in the hands and feet, they got the wound in the side which finished off Christ or at least certified him dead. I'm missing that one; and there's hardly time or occasion for a custard pie to provide it. For I intend to disappear again. A car in which

one can sleep? Van? Caravan? A begging bowl under an
Indian tree? Be your age, Wilf! It is too late for that. I shall
disappear into comfort and security!

Which brings us right up to today. I have taken all the
papers from the chests and built them into a bonfire down
by the river. As I sit at this desk I have only to lift my head
and over the typewriter I can see the pile, a positive
mountain of mostly white paper waiting there—startlingly
white against the dark woods on the other side of the river.
When I've rounded off this manuscript I shall take a can of
paraffin down there, drench the lot and set fire to it—a rite
of passage made out of the detritus, the nail clippings, cut
hair, the worn-away time, unnecessary correspondence,
reviews, theses, financial statements, manuscripts,
interlinears, proofs, the paperweight of a whole life!

Then I shall find Rick and give him this small sheaf of
papers, all that is necessary, all that will be left, all that
means anything to set over against the lying stories, the
partial journals and all the rest. It will be a kind of dying.
Freedom forsooth, freedom quotha.

I am happy, quietly happy. How can I be happy?
Sometimes the experience is like a jewel, exquisite,
sparkling, without words. Sometimes it is calm and
beyond all my ordinary experience, because of its perfect
calmness. I am happy. That's not reasonable, it's a fact.
Either I have broken away from the intolerance which is
impossible, or it has let me go, which is also impossible.

How could I change? But I have changed. Drink, for
example. After more than a quarter of a century of trying I
have now given up drink for good without trying at all! It
may be a perilous thing to write in view of the times the
clown's trousers have fallen down; but I know with
absolute, inward certainty that I have drunk my last drink.

Who knows? With intolerance backed right out of the
light there is room for an unconvenanted mercy like the
one that drives me to give Rick these papers: a mercy
by which those unsatisfactory phenomena, Wilfred
Townsend Barclay and Richard Linbergh Tucker may be

eternally destroyed. Is that what keeps me happy?

Rick is a hundred yards away across the river, flitting from tree to tree like playing Indians. I shall have an audience for my ritual. Now he is leaning against a tree and peering at me through some instrument or other.

How the devil did Rick L. Tucker manage to get hold of a gu